GIVE ME YOUR GOOD EAR

GIVE ME YOUR GOOD EAR

Maureen Brady

Afterword by
JACQUELINE ST. JOAN

SPINSTERS, INK
RD 1, ARGYLE, N.Y. 12809

The characters in this book are fictitious and any resemblance to actual persons is purely coincidental.

Chapter 11 of this novel originally appeared in SO'S YOUR OLD LADY.

ISBN 0-933216-00-9

Library of Congress Catalog Card Number: 78-66097

First edition

Front cover photograph by Rita Hammond

Printed in the United States of America

For my mother and my grandmothers,
and in memory of Elizabeth Brown.

The publishers wish to express gratitude to those generous donors whose contributions helped to create Spinsters, Ink and to make the publication of this book possible.

Special acknowledgement is made to Irena Klepfisz for her fine editorial assistance, and to Harmony Hammond and Marian Roth for assistance with design.

ONE

Do you remember playing crack the whip? I do. I played it all through my childhood and all through my adolescence and all through my young adulthood. My name is Francie Kelly, Frances Catherine Kelly on my birth certificate, and I'm an expert at that game.

We played it in the bog of a cemetery that we used for an ice skating pond in winter. The rest of the year we played it outside the schoolhouse or in old-man Peter's cow pasture or in the clearing by the apple orchard; but where we played it didn't seem to have anything to do with the fact that I always got stuck on the tail end. It was a fast game, the way I saw it. You hung on for all you were worth. The memory runs like a backward spiral in my mind and I can picture a smaller version of myself, my two red pigtails spun out by centrifugal force, my sweaty hands clenched, my lips pursed, my intention—survival. It was hopeless to attempt to control my own direction as the momentum surged out to me, passed hand to hand through the chain. It was horrendous to imagine letting go, how far the thrust might take me, how I would land, face down, skinning my nose, as I sailed, missile-like, across the clay playground dirt. But even worse was to imagine giving in, becoming a slave to the chain, letting the whip crack me. My arm being jerked off, leaving the rest of me to spin away, lopsided: my eyes popping out just as I was cracked backwards, rolling away like two racing marbles.

Child's play, you say. A child's imagination roaming wild. True, but there was also this chain of my grandmother, my mother, and me. My grandmother was a very powerful person. Large, obese actually, but able to make the fat seem proper on her, and vibrant—her lungs were like bellows; when she sang, she quivered, her whole throat and her bosom quivered. I was a little girl with two red pigtails and when I watched her bosom quiver, the hairs on the back of my neck stood up. When she wasn't singing, she was submitting to the role, running the vacuum—all the while letting you know she'd been miscast. Moving my grandfather from one chair to another with his newspaper. And he—an inanimate object, never losing his place. She taught my mother the role better than she knew it herself. Mother made it seem more natural, lost track of when she was acting and when she was living, passed it down without the proper sense of irony. So that's why I know all about how much extra ground the tail has to cover and how hard you have to run, trying to keep up, hoping eventually to surpass and move into another position, and how the fear can grip you, holding you fast even after you've told yourself to let go. That's why long after I'd observed the fact that it was utterly crazy for Ben and me to be anywhere near each other, we could still be found in almost deadly proximity.

It was on the way home from Marblehead that I knew, absolutely, that I had to get out. Ben was rambling on and on, translating the charm of the town into his technician's jargon. He had driven by the first dozen restaurants that I suggested looked okay for lunch, and stopped at the thirteenth only when I had threatened to wet my pants on the seat of his new car.

"Jesus, food is food, babe. We're not likely to find any place that's perfect here," I said.

Up till that moment of the day, Ben had been in a good mood (for him), which is to say he'd been traveling under the illusion that he, with his M.I.T. perspective, was the center of the cosmos.

"Okay, okay. I stopped, didn't I?" His tone made it clear that I had brought him down.

Ben stationed himself at a booth, while I made for the door marked *Ladies.* He headed for *Men* as soon as I returned. He hadn't admitted he had to go but I should have known. One of the things Ben and I had in common was a good deal of bladder anxiety. We'd both been childhood bed-wetters and the fear clings long after the sphincter succumbs to parental horror. I looked around and registered the fact that the exposed light bulbs were going to drive Ben bananas. I noticed the gash in the yellow seat cover on his side of the booth. It reminded me of the plastic dinette chairs in the kitchen where I grew up—a shiny, pearly look for those who have never seen a showcase of designer furniture. I considered switching sides to sit on the gash, knowing that Ben would shrink disgustedly from it as if it were an open wound seeping bacteria. He was taking a long time in the restroom and I wondered if it too was out of toilet paper, if he'd taken a shit before he realized it, if maybe I should go knock on the door and offer to pass through a Kleenex.

For God's sakes, why do I think I have to take care of this man?

He returned, his morose expression telling me he disliked everything around him. Space tight, I read, as he crossed his long legs. He helped the top one over the bottom one with his hand as if they were detached extremities, as though he were making the first move toward tying a knot—a knot which would end up in my stomach for having brought him to this place.

"Let's order and get out of here soon," he said.

"Okay with me. I don't want to hang around. It'll be nice when we get out on the country roads. Look at those colors."

A row of trees surrounded the parking lot of the diner showing off the beauty of autumn. The shorter, delicate yellow poplar stood in the shelter of the tall red maple. The sun shone on both of them and created a harmony that made the air around our booth seem polluted, overcast and dreary. I hated myself for going through the summer and now the fall with Ben's shadow over me.

We might have been having just any ordinary lousy lunch but the need to touch reality forced me to acknowledge that this whole trip had been designed for moving us backward to the time when we had made a similar trip, supposedly in love. We had found an almost perfect restaurant in Mystic and had sat in a booth by the bar. Over and over our eyes had met and triggered a smile in one of us, which then triggered a smile in the other. We had ordered lobsters and I could feel my salivary glands shooting out little juicy sprays, anticipating the butter and the sweet meat.

"You're beautiful," Ben had said. "I love to see you smile."

"It's good to feel so happy," I had said, touching my fingertips to his and watching the message of my touch travel almost instantaneously to his eyes, brightening them.

We ate slowly, moaning and purring and sucking and picking and cracking, keeping track of the other's progress and sensations, laughing and getting drunk on the wine.

"I don't ever want to get to the last piece," I said.

"I know. Why don't we get another one?"

"What a fantastic idea. You know I never would have thought of that. It's like a taboo that's so taken for granted—eating two whole meals in one sitting—that you never even realize it's there. Let's get two more." It became clear to me then that I'd been living with a desire to order two lobsters for myself all my life. When I was a kid, I always had to split one with my brother.

We made it through four lobsters without taking anything for granted. We held each other with our eyes almost constantly and I felt warm and full. Then the restaurant was closing and we went out to the salt breeze and chased each other down the beach on drunk, wobbly legs. In the room we played in the shower, slippery with soap, stopping to kiss and forgetting about the soap, so when my tongue moved down his neck, I got my mouth washed out. We made love laughing, hesitating with due respect each time a gurgle protested from our butter coated insides. I fell asleep, loving the night and him and feeling I'd never be lonely again.

It never works to try to put your relationships in reverse and travel back to "a time when. . ." but it's one of those lessons that is so hard to learn that we learn it, then forget we've learned it, and have to go back and learn it all over again. *Is this an adequate excuse for the fact that I was stuck to Ben and needed help to get away?*

The food was of the truckdriver, diner variety, actually quite good. I anticipated he would have indigestion anyway as a matter of principle, ego investment in the fact of his general disapproval of the place. He popped a Librium just before we got up from the table, then grabbed the car keys and said he'd drive.

In the car, he said, "I want to go straight home. I really feel bad." So we hit the interstate rather than the country roads. I know what "really feel bad" means and hearing it weights my eyelids, making me sleepy and blank and out of touching range. I dislike this state of lethargy intensely, this fog that insulates me from the bright, clear colors of the leaves all around but I just can't keep my eyes open. I just can't stand the fact that there is nothing permissible for me to do but to feel sorry for him. It's not fair to explode, to put myself first when he is feeling bad, when he is needing me. He is working on his head to the tune of seventy dollars a week and he expects me to understand that the sheer effort involved in doing that is enough to justify his anxiety. Whatever is coming out in his therapy, I wouldn't be capable of understanding. He's right about that. He's making my life miserable and I hate him so thoroughly that I don't care to understand anymore. I just want him to know he deserves to be left alone and deserted.

At the entrance to the Mass. Turnpike, we encounter a small traffic jam. He starts to perspire and his wet hands clench the wheel. I try not to notice him but he begins to shake. "Oh God, I'm sick, Francie. I'm scared," he says.

I am afraid. Even though my eyes feel droopy, I am too close. Not out of touching range. I have this creepy feeling of lack of recognition as I wonder, who is this man and what on earth am I doing here?

"What's wrong?" I ask, not wanting to know.

"My heart."

"What about it?" I don't want to be involved but I am a physical therapist and the adrenalin has shot up to that area of my brain where medical knowledge is stored.

"It's off," he says, desperation in his voice. "It goes double, then stops." He has his hand on his chest just like someone in the movies having a real heart attack. His forehead is beady with sweat.

"We can go to an emergency room."

"No, they'll think I'm crazy."

"So what? You'd be sure you're okay."

"Leave me alone, Francie. For God's sake leave me alone. When we get through the toll booth, you drive and I'll sleep in the back seat."

The last time this happened we were in bed and I put my good ear on his chest. Lub dub, lub dub, the heart was beating steady and I told him so but he didn't believe me. He's been checked out by EKG's and all that—cardiac neurosis.

"Just relax. You'll be okay." I wipe his forehead with a tissue. "Don't panic." I am trying to make my voice calm but there is a plaintive wail in it. I can feel the vocal cords all bunched up high in my throat.

When I start to drive he falls asleep very easily in the back seat, curled by his fear into a ball; because we have these modern headrests to prevent whiplash, it is difficult for me to catch a glimpse of him. I would like to forget he is there, to enjoy the drive. I try thinking of old loves and wind up way back in the few snug moments of my childhood.

Always in these moments of fear I go floating to the past. Even at his best, Ben is a lousy, nervous driver. To watch the road, the hazards of cars around us is so frazzling I have to leave the present, to float with the riding motion, jagged as Ben makes it with his nerves. Altogether I must spend a ridiculous ninety percent of the time I am in the car with him transporting myself elsewhere.

I am slumped on the hay floor of our tree hut, my back against the sturdy wall we built. My brother is rolling a cigarette which will make him turn green when we smoke it. Zeke is my boyfriend and Joey's best friend and the three of us talk about when we will be old enough to drive, how we will select our cars; we hold imaginary steering wheels in front of us and make purring motor noises. Sometimes Zeke and I kiss, practicing that skill which we sense will become more important with time. There is no sex in these kisses, only practice at breath control and how stiff to keep the lips.

Ben moves in the back seat, utters a grunting noise. Pig, that's what he is. Never takes his own clothes to the cleaners, relies on me to clean up his urine drippings, splattered and hardened like some protein substance around the toilet bowl. Only in the beginning would he lie for a long time looking at me after we made love, making me feel as if the wonder of it all was holding him entranced. I would trace his body with my eyes closed, his long, long thighs, his jutting pelvic bones. It was the middle of the summer and we would adjust our position a little and feel the cool spots where we had perspired together being exposed to the air. He had a vulnerable look in those moments, pleased with himself at our having climbed to the peaks together—not unlike Zeke's smile when I said, "That was a good one," after a gentle kiss.

It is hard to believe I am thinking of the same person, whose heavy, sleeping breath I can hear behind me. I feel nothing for him. I know he is in pathetic shape, suffering some terrible constriction, and that I should be sorry for him. But I am sorry for myself. My insides are raging: Why me? I want a man who can hold up under the simple conditions of going away for a weekend.

We lost it after the first summer when sex became a night thing—an exercise you do to get off to a sweet sleep. He would roll away from me and go into the bathroom long before the joy should have evaporated. I hated him for washing my smell off. I should have left him then but instead started getting up to wash his smell off too. I kept remembering the flutters he created in my gut when he used to watch me walk across a room and I knew I'd been chosen. I knew he was admiring the way my body moved for me, I knew he was lonely and wanted to draw me close to him. I kept remembering how vast my bed had seemed when I slept only on one side of it, even though the other side was empty. I told myself I'd been a dismal failure with this couple thing because I always expected too much, that it was crazy to think I could have the gap filled without giving up the pleasures of living alone, of reading the whole day Sunday if I felt like it, of driving the country roads instead of the interstate.

He was jarred again into my world by the West Side Highway. "I'm sorry you had to do all the driving, babe."

"That's okay. I don't mind." I was frozen, scared, wanted him to stay asleep. Didn't want him knowing I was leaving him when he was on the verge of going berserk. But he was awake, so I had to muster up an act.

"Do you feel better?"

"Yeah, not good but better."

There is always the danger of forgetting an act is an act. Inside I kept repeating—remember this day was for real, the same as all our other misery—got to get out, drop his hand.

He sat up and watched the city go by. I felt like a cab driver. My passenger was a stranger. I would have liked to drop him off and go home to my own life. We went to the garage. He was revived enough to want to eat. He was becoming his more relaxed self again but I was beyond that seduction. I'd refuse to put my blinders on again. The horse runs round and round the same track, only to drop from exhaustion in the end. The question that made me feel shaky-weak and afraid to look squarely at Ben was the only one left—*how* to break away?

TWO

I was having my coffee alone while Ben carefully attended to his bowels, a prerequisite to getting the work day off right. You had to feel sorry for him. Nothing came naturally to him except perhaps drawing straight lines on a fresh sheet of white paper. And yet when I thought of leaving him, my stomach knotted up into a ball and all his needs started piling up in a stack in my mind. I wandered into a schedule, a warning plan. Today, Monday—"I'm very unhappy. Do you think I need a shrink?" Tomorrow, Tuesday—"It's hopeless, baby. I know you don't think you intend to, but you intimidate me. I feel like the grass growing and at the end of every week you mow me down again. . . ."

It is not fair that I've been given this thorough, comprehensive education in how to acquire a man and keep him, and not a clue as to how to leave him. My home economics teacher in the eighth grade—I fell in love with her dark, wavy hair, her sensitive brown eyes and I hung on every word she said—she actually made up specific, detailed lesson plans on luring him, holding him, and keeping him happy. Then she ended the period with a blissful smile when she should have been teaching us how to escape this horrendous relationship she'd gotten us into.

"You might as well make the best of it," Mother always said, *it* being whatever life circumstances you found yourself stuck with. She spent almost all of her life trying to live that statement, and I, being an eager achiever, took this education much too seriously.

There were the days when we'd come home from school, throw down our books and run out to play. We'd come back in again when Mom called us for dinner. It was like hearing your name in a song, the way her voice carried and echoed. "Még-an, Frán-cie, Jó-ey." Dad would be sitting at the table with his beer and she would be buzzing around the stove. He'd be wearing his dirty work clothes but his sleeves would be rolled up and you could tell from the pink of his skin that he'd just finished scrubbing up. From his hands up to his elbows the hairs would be damp, dew damp, the kind you have to touch to be sure, and his face and neck would be damp, too, and you could see the dark ring around his khaki shirt collar which he always got wet.

"Oh, Daddy, can I have some beer?" I'd ask.

"Go wash up for dinner," Mom would say.

"Then can we have some?"

"Do as your mother says," he'd say, stern enough to make you afraid he was mad at you.

We'd all three rush to the bathroom and roll up our sleeves and grab for the soap. Whoever got it first would rub for what seemed like ages, building up a lather the same way Dad did, while the other two begged and pleaded with hands cupped beneath it to be next. You might think we were a very clean family but actually that was our only cleaning ritual besides the weekly bath, which took place on a rotating schedule, posted next to the kitchen sink, that told you who got the clean water, who got once-used water, and who got twice-used water. I didn't mind being after Megan because she never got very dirty (Joey and I even tried to plead the case that Megan should be removed from the bath schedule completely as a sort of punishment for her saintly cleanliness), but bathing after Joey was like sitting in stirred-up creek slime.

I took for granted that this was a universal family practice, this bathing in threes—or can you imagine if you were one of seven? Much later I found out that we'd been saving water for the animals and the eggs; we weren't "gentleman farmers."

Six anxious little hands up to the elbows and three faces down to the collars can make a sink look like the alluvial shores at the ass end of a river. "I hope you're not making a mess in there," Mom would call out just as we were drying off, and then we'd have to get into the argument over who made the mess and who should clean it up. "It wasn't me," Megan would say. She might have been the cleanest one but I'd venture to say somewhat objectively that she could still make a mess just as well as anyone else. "Well, I didn't do it all," Joey would say, preparing for that accusation before anyone could make it. I, who might best be characterized as the family saint, if you didn't know that I was only interested in avoiding the clamor of harsh words, would say, "I'll clean up this half. Come on, Joey, you do the other side."

But he'd say, "No, Megan did at least a third. She has to help too."

Then she'd take over, swishing the washcloth around his side with her nose stuck up in the air to tell you that she didn't make the mess but she'd clean up after us, just as Mom did, because she was a half-Mom and we were such sniveling little brats we couldn't possibly be expected to do it for ourselves.

Back in the kitchen, we'd stand in front of Dad with our juice glasses hold at a slant for him to pour half full with beer. Knowing enough to hold my glass at just the right angle for a one inch head gave me the feeling of being a professional, right up there with Dad. It was one of the special pleasures of my life to take my glass to my chair and to arrange myself like him, my elbows on the table, my two hands caressing the glass, turning it from time to time and watching the yellow bubbles rise. We'd sit there in silence mostly, drinking our beer, feeling it tickle our throats. If one of us would make a face, he'd catch it and pretend to be insulted. "Ah ha, making faces at my beer. You don't like it, eh?"

Then Mom would pass around the plates and we'd eat.

The female contingent had a schedule for washing and drying the dishes. The one who wasn't on that night could go in the sitting room and listen to a radio program with Dad and Joey. If it was Mom's turn and she so much as said, "Oh, what a day. I'm tired." Dad would butt in and say, "Okay girls, you do the dishes tonight. Your mother's tired."

"But it's her turn," I'd say.

Then she'd insert feebly, "That's okay. I'm not too tired for the dishes."

"Leave your mother alone. You heard me. I said you girls would do the dishes tonight." His face would redden and his weight would lean forward toward you and you knew better than to say any more even though your voice screamed inside you, "But we have a schedule and it's none of your business. She could offer to trade with one of us."

After they'd gone into the sitting room, Megan and I would work listlessly at the chore, speaking back and forth in rasping whispers.

"There ought to be a law against it," Megan said, repeating one of Dad's favorite lines, her upper lip curled toward her nose.

"Yeah. We might as well not have this stupid schedule. He doesn't know beans. What gives him the right? Just because he's so big he thinks he's King Tut."

"I'd like to punch him. Why does he have to be so mean?"

"I don't know. I hate him."

Mom would always manage to sneak in to take a look at how we were doing. "Francie, that dish isn't clean. Look, if you're going to do it, do it right."

"I don't care," I'd say, punctuating my detachment with a careless flip of the dishrag. "If you don't like the way I do it, you can do it yourself." Although our talk was mostly about him, we weren't about to let her off the hook. After all, we were the children. That's why we couldn't fight with him. What was her excuse? Why didn't she stand up to him, tell him to stay out of it, instead of acting as though he'd cast a spell over her, as though he'd stepped in front of her and made her invisible? Once she'd taken on that invisible quality she seemed to think no one would ever notice that she'd been the original source of the trouble.

After the dishes were done, we'd all troop down to the cellar to grade the eggs. Mom's job was to wash them with lye while they were still in the baskets. Dad candled them with a special light to look for blood spots and then placed them on spoonlike receptacles which rotated around the center of the grader. If the egg was heavy, the spoon dipped low and would be knocked off by the first knocker-offer. Lighter eggs went on to the second and third knocker-offers and pee-wees sometimes went all the way around back to Dad. The three of us stood according to age, and picked off the ones that fell into our compartments and packed them in crates. Megan had large and I had medium. Joey was lucky to have small because he had the fewest eggs to pack and the fun of guessing whether the pee-wees would make it or not. On the good nights you could get a real nice feeling of our being a family doing this chore. The cellar had a good smell of damp earth from the other end where there was no floor, the grader made a pleasant hum, and the task took enough concentration so that no one talked much. I watched the eggs coming round and tried to guess which place they would fall into and I was right so many times and wrong so many times. There was the click of the knocker-offer pushing the egg into my compart-ment, then the egg rolling down the gentle slope of wood and crashing into my other eggs that I hadn't put away yet. Never breaking. It was extraordinary. They made a light, smacking noise. Inside, I would feel each crash, magnified a hundred times, sure disaster. I'd pick up two, my arms would swing to the crate, drop them into place, but my eyes would return way before the arms, watching for the next crash. They were so fragile, you could practically see through the shells. How they could absorb that smack as if they were marbles was to me one of the mysteries of life. Same as I survived Dad's fist slamming down on the table over and over, though I was always convinced it would shatter me.

Of course if you so much as tapped them on the lip of your compartment, the eggs would break. Megan and I usually managed to break a few on the nights we needed reparation for having been bullied into the dishes. I felt like a child laborer then and my speed would be picked up by my fury so that my compartment was always empty, waiting for the next egg, and while I waited, tapping my foot impatiently at the lousy, slow rhythm of the grader, I would plan a speech requesting a raise in my stinking fifteen-cent allowance.

Even on those nights, though, after the hour or so it took to do all the eggs, I would realize that Mom had the worst job of all and begin to feel sorry for her. She had to wear heavy rubber gloves and stand in front of a huge double sink with the hot water steaming in her face. You could either look away from her and pretend that we were all better because we weren't stuck with that job, or you could watch her and wonder why she put up with it. Mostly, if I watched her, my sorrow would change to hate.

Dad was very much like Ben in the way he could turn a good day into a bad day on the basis of just about nothing. When Dad let me sit up there at the table with him, sipping my beer and watching the sun come down through the screen door, squinting when it got to the angle that could blind you, I'd feel I was a real person, his companion and his daughter. I knew that he was bigger and that his glass was taller and that the head of his beer was at the top of his glass while mine was at the middle, but none of those things mattered. What mattered was the silent camaraderie that gave me such a sunny feeling about him, a feeling that fooled me time and time again so that I never could quite believe he was the same father who was liable in the next moment to be spitting harsh commands and pounding his fist on the table. When he'd turn into that other man, my stomach would involute and shrivel, trying to pull back from him. I would feel sick and have to concentrate on keeping the churning contents of my stomach where they were because I hated to vomit. I would squint and then cross my eyes and stare at the tip of my nose until I got a little dizzy and then I could better pretend he wasn't there.

Ben and I, too, had those times when we sat across a table and appeared to be equals sharing a dusk together or a late-night snack or a weekend breakfast. Just as I'd be easing into a sense of comfort about it, feeling, this is nice, we can sit and have a conversation like two mature adults, even allow for differences in opinion, Ben would stand up to demonstrate the difference in our sizes. He was twelve inches taller than I. He'd pick these moments as a predator bides his time for a good meal. He had to take his opinion and stand over me with it and if I didn't acquiesce immediately, he'd do the demonstration of how his voice was louder and lower. Then he'd trot off to the bathroom. He'd usually come back from the bathroom ready to fight. I was too old for staring at my nose cross-eyed. So what did I do? I'd feel that same disastrous churning in my stomach and I'd step right into Mom's shoes, silent sneakers, and pull my extremities in close, hoping to be small and unobtrusive enough to be considered absent. How long, after all, could he argue with himself? Once I had myself balled up, small as I could be, out of his range, I could live out his wrath as a spectator. I might have been at the zoo watching a restless baboon. I felt the same confidence then that Mom must have felt when she knew with a time-tested sureness that all it took for her to be in control was some subtle gesture that could be interpreted as kneeling down. The confidence included, too, the knowledge that at that moment Ben was nothing more than an overinflated bag, empty inside but for the wind, and if one wanted to pop him, one could do it simply enough with no more than a straight pin and then he'd be gone; the air would be completely expelled, and he would be gone. There is nothing quite so useless as the flabby piece of rubber left in your hand after you have popped a balloon. Was it this fear of being left with nothing or was it the fear of leaping suddenly into the territory of—I am significant, you shut up and listen to me for a change —and finding him deaf, dumb, and blind to me that kept me silent on the sidelines?

I remember the nights when my wish was for Mom to strike out at my father, for her to grow large and to fill with rage. But she stayed small. We all stayed small with fear and behaved sanely, you might say. Those were the nights when Dad went to town after he had brought the eggs in—went to town and forgot to come home for dinner.

If I was out playing with Debbie and Zeke, who lived down the road on the next farm, and Mrs. Lester called them in, my alarm system would go off at the sound of her voice because normally we ate earlier than they did. I felt as if my heart was a gong and she struck it once for each syllable of their names. The clanging vibrated through my limbs scaring me like the fire drill bells at school. I'd start home then, even though Mother hadn't called yet. In my memory it seems like all those nights were one, although I know there were many. The feelings were always the same: I walked slowly, my eyes on the path I was making through the tall grass in front of me. I looked back at Debbie and Zeke running the other way. It was too late to say, "Maybe I could come to your house for supper. Want to ask your mother?" I visualized them running in through the back door, running right up to where their dad sat and jumping up, scrambling all over him and his fat belly. There were five more kids in their family and when he came home from work they all crawled up on him, up his legs and into his arms. I'd seen it many times. He sometimes reminded me of an ant hill. But even if I'd been there, I wouldn't have crawled up on him. He wasn't my father.

Maybe Mr. Lester got home early, I thought. Even though they had a small farm, Mr. Lester had to drive the Coca-Cola truck to feed all those mouths. I pulled a shoot from the ground and sucked the sweet end of it, heartened by the possibility of his being early.

But he wasn't early. You could tell by the sun that it was getting late. I scuffed my feet, kicking up little puffs of dirt, and then I reached the place where I could see that the car was gone. It was a '43 Chevrolet with running boards and I could never think of it without remembering the day when Dad had been backing out the driveway and Mom had come running after him, saying, "Stephen, please. Please don't go. You've had too much already. Come back in and you can have another drink here." She'd gotten up on the running board so that her desperate face was right in his ear and he'd backed the car out and tried to push her off with his elbow where the window was rolled down, but she'd clung like a leech until he started going forward. She had finally just dropped off, stepping back. Like a leaf dropping off a tree—you couldn't be sure of the exact moment the separation had occurred even though you had seen it. My heart had been thumping wildly against my chest. She had dropped off so easily that I had been sure that she would be run over or that he would turn the corner fast, whirling her off into the ditch.

I stopped at the pig pen and watched Hortense, my favorite, for a few minutes. Hortense, with all her ornery bulk, made frequent, subtle escapes and took on all five of us before she'd get fooled back into her pen. I threw a few pebbles at her. You could get a sense of how hopeless it was to try to argue with Dad by throwing pebbles at Hortense. They just bounced off. She didn't move her snout from the trough. "Who do you think you are, anyway? You're a little nobody," was the message.

Walking across the lawn, I prayed, "Please God, let him just be gone for a few minutes to pick something up. Let him come home for supper before it's too late."

I went in the kitchen, letting the screen door slam behind me, on purpose, because it made me feel I was really there.

"How many times do I have to tell you? DON'T SLAM THAT DOOR!"

"Okay, sorry."

"If you only knew how that gets on my nerves. Twenty-five times a day. Whap, whap. I feel like it's beating me."

"Sorry. It's done already. I can't take it back. What do you want me to do? Go out and come in again?"

I could see that Mom was in one of those moods where she was sorry to be alive, but she held her spine straight as she drifted away from me, lifting the lids from the pots on the stove, checking the dinner. She was always efficient with her pot holders, even when she was upset.

Her hair was long, coming down almost to her waist when she brushed it out. It was a rich, earth brown, and though it was pure in the portrait of her that hung in the living room, the hairs were now turning grey too often to be plucked out. She brushed it each morning on the porch. She was beautiful then, when the long strands draped down her back and over her shoulders and the sun lit on her and her green eyes looked out calmly on the lawn. It was the only time of the day she took for herself and I liked to watch her whenever I had the chance. She seemed to daydream while she brushed, and even after all the knots were gone, she continued to brush some more, bringing out the natural oils, she claimed. Then slowly, methodically, she'd pick the hairs out of the brush and leave a hair ball on the porch rail for the birds to use in their nests. Finally, she'd go up to her room to braid and twist her hair so that it all ended up on top of her head, held there with her combs. She even slept with it that way.

Wrinkles were set in lines around her eyes and across her forehead and the corners of her mouth turned down just slightly when she wasn't smiling. Her hands were wrinkled too. In the summer they were speckled with large, brown freckles and the skin had a thick, horny look to it. Though they were good, useful hands that could do just about anything, I thought it a shame she didn't have slender hands because if there was one thing she really wanted to do, it was to play the piano. If you watched her when she didn't know you were looking, there was a sort of sad droop to her face, a wistful turning out of her lips. I magnified her expression, dramatically whenever I was disappointed, sticking my lower lip out and curling it down till I could feel it touching my chin, and she couldn't bear that look on me. "If you don't stop that, I'll cut your lip off," she'd say. If she knew you were watching her, she put on a regular face, one which said, "I can smile at just about anything."

"When's dinner?" I asked.

"Soon. Wash up and then call Megan and Joey in."

I hadn't meant to ask but it came out anyway. "Where's Dad?" It came out sounding like a routine, irrelevant question.

"He went to town. If he doesn't come home soon, we'll eat without him." Her tone was the same as mine. We always used that middle-C mode to create the illusion that he had no effect on our lives. He'd brought in the eggs first, hadn't he? Well, that was all we expected of him.

I had been sitting at the table, watching her move back and forth from the stove to the sink. Then I got up and set the table without being asked, to try to make Dad's absence up to her. She put the supper in the oven, where it would eventually dry out, and then she sat down, her good ear anxiously perked towards the driveway. Mother had the same bad ear as Grandma Gerty—the left one—a problem, for she had to sit with her good ear away from Dad in order to be near the stove. Dad hated it when she'd say, "What?"

When Megan and Joey came in complaining of starvation, she took the supper back out of the oven. We were eating in silence until Joey said, "Why don't you call the American Legion?" The statement smacked like an avalanche of eggs rolling too fast, hitting too hard at the bottom of a hill too steep and I felt myself cringing for Mother.

"Never mind, Joey. Just eat. You were so hungry."

I'd been to the American Legion bar a couple of times Times when we all went to town together and Dad stopped off there and Mom let us come with her to pick him up. The place was so dark you could hardly make out who was who, but you'd hear Dad's voice. "Hey there," he'd say, and then, to the man on the next stool, "You know my kids? You know the girls, Megan and Francie, and this is my son, Joey." The man would remark on how rapidly we'd grown. There was sawdust on the floor and a long row of whiskey bottles on the wall and a dart board, which he wouldn't let us play with. A hum of low voices went on and on, steady as a rocking chair and I could imagine how you could lose track of the time with that drone going on around you. Joey was right. Mom should just call him and remind him it was dinner time. But I knew. I knew she'd done that before, more than once, and that he'd gotten mad and stayed even longer and not come home until after we were in bed.

No one was very hungry. "Come on now, eat, all of you. Eat your peas, too, Joey."

Joey puckered up his lips and pleaded with his eyes to be spared from the peas.

We all heard the car then, our ears alert as if we were a family of rabbits. We busied ourselves with the food. He let the screen door slam. I saw Mom flinch with the whapping noise. He stood a moment, swaying, before he took his seat at the end of the table. He was a very large man. Not that tall and not fat either, but when he stood there, he seemed to loom over us all. His face was slack, so slack you'd think he might drool. His thick hair was messed up, as if he'd just gotten up from a night of sleeping without getting undressed. His eyes were bloodshot.

"I'll get your dinner," Mother said, the caution in her voice reminding us to keep quiet, as if we would have dared to say anything.

"Well, does everyone have a clean plate?" His voice boomed, much too loud for the room. It bounced off the cabinets. "Have you been behaving for your mother?"

"Yes, Daddy," Megan replied, sitting straight, her voice shaky. I was just as scared to answer him as she was not to. His eyes scanned the room as if he were looking for something to harp on. I tried not to look at him, but found myself darting glances anyway, keeping track of him. It was in his eyes, the thing that held us frozen to our seats while little fragments of prayers shot through our minds. It was a leer that searched for something or someone to pounce on and you knew that if he ever pounced, he would never be able to stop. He would pound and pound and pound until all the violence was gone. I remembered him pulling on the cabinets once when he was drunk and looking for a glass. Holding the handles with both hands and slamming the doors shut and then pulling them open with all his weight leaning back, over and over till you were sure they would come off the wall, falling, crushing him. And I knew that whatever it was inside of him that made him do that had a way of hurting him because the look on his face was the same one of unbearable pain that you have when you stub your toe real bad and you rock back and forth and it hurts so much you don't know what to do.

When he dropped his head down on his arms at his place at the table, we breathed again. We knew he was asleep almost instantly. We got up quietly from the table as if afraid of disturbing some fierce monster and tiptoed into the sitting room. We didn't have to do the dishes those nights or even the eggs. We'd lie on the floor and try to concentrate on Roy Rogers or Hopalong Cassidy on the radio. I'd never be able to get my mind off him, though, the way he had looked when he stood in the doorway and what would happen if his arms came flinging out at me some night. Even the sounds on the radio, the sounds of a posse riding out, made me nervous, made me worry that it wasn't safe to lie flat out as I was on the floor, that a stampede could tear right over me, grinding me into dust.

Mom of course had to pretend she wasn't scared of him. She had to touch him. She had to lead this grumbling hulk of flesh through the sitting room and up the stairs and plop him on the bed. I imagined her standing there looking down on him after he was laid out and my hands would clench up into fists for her, but I knew she was probably taking his shoes off.

How many times had Ben left me lying beside him with my sweaty hands fisted while he snored? He had the ability to pass out without even being drunk. Having barked out all his anger in my direction, he'd recline flat out and zonk before I'd gotten my feelings formed into words. I could always work up a brave and righteous speech then, as long as he was unconscious.

THREE

Often I walked to work. Today the sun reached the sidewalk in patches. I took long strides between them and slowed my pace to a meander whenever I reached one. It was a tease, that sun, reminding me of Debbie knocking on the screen door of my childhood and calling, "Can Francie come out and play?"

No, no, Francie can't go out and play. She's living in a wretched relationship and she can't get away. Her own ghosts are haunting her—boo. She's scared and she's cold, almost numb, almost can't feel anything anymore but she can feel the beams of sunlight and she remembers lighter days.

I had my coffee and doughnut and said my morning greetings like an automaton. The social aspect of my work was the part most easily affected by my mood. The work itself called up my resources, demanded that I be there, as strong a presence as possible. This required a major readjustment from the kind of passive morning behavior Ben could tolerate. However, once in the gym, I managed to escape, if not from myself, at least from him. I would be safe for the next eight hours.

"How are you today, Gwyn?"

"I used to be a dancer," she said.

I tried to do some exercises with her. I asked her to straighten her leg. She stared at my mouth as if she could lip-read. I repeated my request. She stared at my hair. I wondered about what she was like before her stroke. She had been found on the floor in her apartment. Her chart recorded her suffering from malnutrition. Had she thought she was going to die, there on the floor, before anyone broke in and found her? Had they broken through police locks or did her super have a key?

I tried to will her to concentrate on her leg. "Gwyn, kick your leg up here and touch my hand." I held my hand out to where her leg should easily reach. She reached out her unparalyzed hand and touched mine. "Your leg," I said, holding her hand.

I wondered if her spirit had withered with her body, if she was already so far into the twilight zone that she was enjoying drifting downhill, fading into oblivion. If that was the case, I wondered why I was bugging her to recover. Because that was my job; besides there was no way to know for sure what she wanted.

I decided to try a more natural approach. Stand her up and maybe she'd walk by reflex. Maybe she'd dance. "What kind of a dancer were you, Gwyn?"

"A fancy dancer," the squeaky, rarely-used voice returned, and her eyes focused on mine for a few seconds, clear and proud. I had been straining to imagine that she wasn't always seventy five, going on eighty-five, looking like ninety-five. She weighed maybe eighty pounds, just a rail with a chest the shape of a young, asthmatic boy. She had those indented eye sockets that make you realize how close to a circle the eyeball really is. Her bones protruded through her skin, which had none of the warm, softening protection of fat. She had ulcers over most of her bony prominences from the pressure of her eighty pounds lying against a mattress with little reason to stir. Her white hair was wig-dry.

She used to be a fancy dancer.

She was walking along, holding the bar, looking light footed, until she stopped and crumpled into my arms in slow motion. She felt as if she weighed three hundred pounds. It took all my adrenalin to carry her dead weight to her wheelchair, two feet away. "Get a doctor," I called to Dan, the other therapist working in the gym.

There she sat with those eyes wide open, staring out of those deep sockets, seeing the absolute zero. Ghost white, no pulse but my own, beating rapidly as I felt for hers. Should I close her eyes? Why me? I had only met her the week before. It seemed too personal. Why doesn't the doctor come and pronounce her dead before her body falls forward and collapses on me? It suddenly didn't seem right for her to remain dead in the position I had given her. Come on Gwyn, give one last twitch or spasm to assert yourself. Remind me you were a person, a dancer. Point your toes, do something.

Nothing. Complete passivity. She'd gone out without a complaint, without a request. Dan came back with the doctor. "Put her on the mat," she said. Dan and I lifted her quickly, professionally, tight grasps on the key points of her skeleton, and she woke up. The flattened, feeble artery slowly gained momentum and began pulsating half life back to the diseased brain, the broken skin and the protruding bones. Her eyes focused on my hair.

"Do you feel all right, Gwyn?"

"Oh yes, I just fell asleep."

It's not so easy to die of old age.

We sent her back upstairs to her bed but all morning the sunken eye sockets, the blankness in her eyes, were before me; I felt myself affected by the urge to see life in her. I took a walk on my lunch hour to get away from her but she stayed with me the way flashes of a dream can follow you for years. Her eyes lighting on mine, sparkling, coming, for that moment, out of the shadow of her dark, untouchable life, and in the next moment, gone. I walked the streets and I saw doors— doors as closed as Gwyn's mind—but no place was right for me. I had keys to Ben's but I didn't belong there. I still had my own apartment but it was nearly empty since I'd moved most of my things to Ben's. I'd only kept it because some part of me had always maintained that Ben was too much of a bastard to imagine living my life with. I could go there; it was in walking distance, but no one would be there, no one but me. And I'd sit in front of the window and watch for life signs in the apartments across the backyard as I'd done before Ben. And it would get me nowhere. But mainly I avoided going there because my legs felt so listless I couldn't imagine climbing the stairs.

What is it like to crack-up or break-down? And why is one up and one down? I thought perhaps I was broken down but no, that was something you did all at once and my condition had grown in me like a slow-spreading tumor—metastatic, lethal, repressed anger. As I walked down the street I imagined each door to be the door to a mental hospital and fantasized myself knocking, still intact, a presentable young woman. The attendant opening the door, starting to speak to me as if I were a visitor but stopping, his mouth gaping, his eyes glaring, first astonishment, then horror, as he views my body oozing and transforming from the shape of flesh and bones to the form of an amoeba, indistinct and difficult to remove from the doorway. He will call the doctor, who will recognize me as a blur of a woman who needs help. She— please God, let the doctor be a she—will give me tiles to make an ashtray and a solitary room with crayons so I can write on the walls and escape this life of mine. I will find my spirit in the purple crayon.

But I was much too uptight. I didn't have the breakdown, just the urge. It takes a certain looseness to let yourself unravel all at once and I didn't have it and wasn't likely to acquire it overnight either. I couldn't even really get angry.

I walked on, stopped in front of the playground, and through the fence watched the two boys in the corner, the one in the red jacket sitting astride the other and holding his arms pinned down and bouncing on the writhing body beneath him. The loser shook his head of straight, blond hair back and forth and screamed curses at his attacker, his face blotched red with anger. I felt the wires of the fence cutting into my fingers and discovered I was gripping it as if I were getting ready to shake it down. The truth is I was explosively angry. I just couldn't get it out.

"She's got a pleasant temperament," they said, "but just watch out you don't make her too mad—she has a ferocious temper." They—Mother and Father. I don't know which one of them put it in those words first, but when I heard myself being described that way, the shame flushed hot on my face and I wanted to disappear. If they were afraid of me, they needn't have been, for the barrier was nailed in solid behind the memory of my ferocious eight-year-old self.

It had been one of those warm, summer days when I'd been perfectly happy playing Wild West before Megan had come home. I had my prisoner tied securely to the porch rail. Poor Joey, always the prisoner; he played the bad guy because he was smaller and I could always catch him.

Megan was a tall, slender girl at nine and a half and one of her tall, slender friends was with her when she came up the driveway. All my friends seemed to be short, plump, and eight. I walked up to her and little lady Linda in my sloppy, tomboy clothes with my holster slung casually around my hips and asked, "Can I play with you?" I had all the likely responses lined up in my mind already—"No, you're too young" or "You don't like girls' games" or "We don't shoot caps"—and I could feel the tightening of my stomach and the setting of my mouth to keep my bottom lip from quivering as it had a tendency to do when I was about to cry. I took such pains never to cry over her. I wanted to scream, "You make me into a tomboy. Let me play with your friends and I'll be a lady. I adore ladies. Can I help it if I got a blue ribbon for winning the broad jump? I didn't mean to win, I jumped too far by accident." But I would never scream at her. She was the princess, the sacred, mysterious lady to be wooed, and always I had the idea in the back of my mind, if I don't tattle or be a crybaby, some day she'll recognize me. Me, the hidden princess under the cowboy suit.

"Close your eyes and hold out your hand. We have a game to play with you," she said.

Joey was yelling from the other end of the porch. "Francie, untie me. I can't get this knot loose and I don't want to play anymore." He was missing three front teeth and probably getting rope burns on his gums, but I didn't care about him. They wanted to play with me.

I closed my eyes and hastily held out my hand with great expectation. I felt something small, round, light, slightly warm, harmless, being placed in my hand. "Now, squeeze hard," Megan commanded. I squeezed for all I was worth, wanting badly to please her, and the bird's egg crumpled easily, oozing gooky, slimy, nauseating raw egg on my hand, and dripping down like a runny nose. She and little lady Linda having a great giggle over the stupid fool who would squash a freshly laid bird's egg in her hand. Great joke. I hated them.

For a minute I felt so bad I didn't know they were laughing. Then I lunged at Megan, wiping some of the egg onto her hand. She went into the kitchen to wash it off, holding the screen door for Linda and then slamming it in my face. I went in and stood across the room and watched them laugh. Very funny. Ha, ha. That's when I lost my mind or, as they say, "my temper." I got this reckless feeling that I could do anything I wanted. The kitchen was large and we were separated by a table in the middle of the room. They weren't paying any attention to me and although there were no limits to what I could do, I was frozen to the spot because they weren't noticing me. Finally Megan turned to me as though she had forgotten, now remembered that I had been a party in this game. I took the gun from my holster and hurled it with the strength of a gorilla at her head. It caught her right in the corner of her left eye and I felt the impact of the throw as if it were equivalent to the thrust of my exploded anger.

Then I relaxed with relief because the anger was gone, uncaged, and I was both sorry and glad that I had hurt her, and more, scared her. I had seen her look—first the smile of disbelief and then the panic freezing her face around that smile. I watched the blood spurt from her eye and mix with her tears, and I felt the hot tears running down my own cheeks. I just stood there and she just stood over the sink splattering red drops. Linda must've called my mother because she came, and then my father came, and I was still feeling the blood drip from my eyes in the form of tears as I lay across my Father's lap. He sat on the toilet seat and struck my bottom, furiously, without counting, without gauging his strength. His striking hands reminded me of how it had been to let my arm throw, hard as it could, with good aim too. I knew he had no control over what he was doing and I doubted if he would ever stop. How could I have struck the princess?

As it turned out, I was saved by her royal highness because Mom had inspected the cut and needed to use the bathroom for bandaging it up. Even a spanking didn't take priority over the princess getting in to use the bathroom. What a beautiful child she was. They had to take her to the hospital then, and she was already clean and wearing a nice dress.

I retreated to my favorite tree in the backyard with my shame. I smiled at my victory and then felt even more ashamed. I remembered the time a rabid fox had come down from the woods, vicious, growling so that the saliva in his mouth seemed to gurgle, running around in a frenzy, attacking whatever he could get his teeth into. Mom and Dad had told us about rabies turning normal foxes crazy. That's how I had felt with the gun, as if I had a disease that made me do it. I shuddered with the memory. Then I prayed that Megan wouldn't be blind.

She wasn't. The stitches led right up to the outside corner of her eye. I followed them carefully to where they ended but I couldn't make my eyes move over the next eighth of an inch to meet hers. I kept my head down most of the time, openly displaying my shame. "I'm sorry," I mumbled. She didn't say anything.

She was at no loss for words, however, when people asked what had happened. She seemed unaware that her straight-forward presentation of the facts incriminated me. "Francie threw her cap gun at me and almost knocked my eye out. I have six stitches and I was lucky I didn't lose my eye."

I could feel the eyes of others looking down on me as if I were a monster. I could feel the reddening of my face and I would set my bottom lip. "What about what Megan did to me?" I wanted to say, but I stayed silent, holding my bottom lip with tight determination. Guilty. Humiliated. Better to make yourself numb than ever to let the rage boil over and possess you.

I worked through the afternoon, losing myself to the needs of those whose disabilities glared so visibly in contrast to mine. If I went to the door of a mental hospital, what could I say that would convince them that my life was oozing away inside of me?

I took off a half-hour early so I could get home and change clothes and get out again before Ben got there. I caught myself literally tiptoeing around the apartment looking for my jeans. "You're really crazy," I said to myself. "He's not even here." Still, I hurried. I had to write him a note explaining where I'd be so he wouldn't have to worry that I was out strumming up someone else's cock. "If he comes through that door right now, I'll stab him with the pencil," I thought.

The note read: "Ben, gone to have dinner with Lisa, then C.R. group at Joan's, W. 92 St. Back around 12. Love, Francie." The love was false—habit—but I left it. An erasure would be too conspicuous. I balanced the note against the salt shaker. The tumbler in the first lock clicked. Too late. I froze. Tumbler number two—a click of finality.

"Hi."

"Hi, I just left you a note."

"Where're you going?"

"To my women's group."

"Oh."

"How come you're home so early?" I asked.

"Because I felt lousy."

"Oh, sorry."

"Why don't you sit down and stay a while?" he said.

"I told Lisa I'd meet her after work for dinner."

"What about me?"

"What about you?"

"You could at least stay home until your meeting and spend some time with me."

"Come on, Ben. Let's not do that number. You know you're going to take a nap and all I'd do is sit around waiting for you to wake up."

Jesus Christ, how could he succeed in making me feel guilty when I knew damn well he only wanted me there so he could sleep a little sounder. Boomerang, he bounced the guilt back at me.

"You've got a guilty look on your face," he said. "You're involved with someone else, aren't you?"

"No."

He raised his voice. "You are. I know it. You were trying to sneak out before I got home."

My voice was surprisingly calm. "You can't make me be involved with someone else just by telling me I am."

"God, Francie, listen to yourself. You don't even deny it."

"I said no."

I was supposed to wrap myself around him and rub reassurance into him with caresses. Even if I had tried to explain, he wouldn't have understood why my women's group seemed the same to him as another man.

"It's hard to believe when you don't defend yourself anymore than that," he said, his voice sour.

"I've got to go. I'll talk to you when I get home." My voice was cracking. My fist was clenched so hard around the pencil that my hand was shaking. A split-second clip of my arm hurling the gun at Megan's eye ran through me and I dropped the pencil so that it rolled to the middle of the table.

The heavy, steel door met the frame with a single, firm thud and I heard him flip the locks from the inside. The mirror by the elevator showed my face splotched red, just like the little boys' in the playground.

FOUR

As a child I had the same nightmare over and over again. The rabid fox snarling and drooling, meeting me face to face on the path in the woods, his eyes fogged over, crazed. I try to woo him with a gentle smile, hoping to breed benevolence while my skin crawls and my hairs stand straight up. He attacks, his fangs sink, two long, sharp claws in the back of my neck, spread chills through my body. His grip stops my breath, killing me with fear. I throw him off, running into the woods, away from the path, only to find myself in his territory. The roots of the trees trip me. I thought they were my friends. No. His. My scream pierces my ears, waking me. Before going back to sleep, I would try so hard to evoke the right image to finish the dream. The image of my dad, holding the gun steady, one shot, the fox carcass at my feet, not so big after all. So many times Dad wasn't there. Only the fox again, the fangs, metal-cold and gripping. I would wake again, sit up straight in bed and remind myself, "Only a dream, only a dream." I would try for the fantasy in which the fox responded to my benevolent smile, his glazed eyes clearing, his growl turning into a playful whimper, an invitation for my hand to run through his fur. I would put my heart and soul into that fantasy and it still would not convince me. The nightmare kept me on edge, readied, with the sheet pulled up over the crawling threat of the goose bumps on the back of my neck, so that when the worst night came, it seemed as if I'd always known it would.

It was one of those nights that Dad didn't come home for dinner. We'd been through our ritual of waiting, then eating and waiting, ostensibly ignoring the empty place at the head of the table while actually being consumed by it. Snatching glances at the shiny yellow dinette chair, imagining the whereabouts of its missing occupant. I envisioned him sitting on the stool, one elbow on the bar, heels hooked on the rungs, mesmerized by the hum of the low voices.

We all ate lethargically, pushing the food around on our plates, indecisive about which forkful of punishment to take first; when someone said "yuck" there were nods all the way round, except for Mom refraining.

He didn't come home. Not while we did the dishes, not even when the storm came and we got out the candles in case the power should go out. We had those thunderstorms often in Otis. The rain came down hard, you could hear it running off the gutters from the roof, sounding like a waterfall, and the lightning burst in through the windows so fast it could stab you in the heart, you couldn't anticipate it. Joey and I talked about how fast we could fill a can with earthworms for bait if only it weren't so late and Mom would let us go out to the garden. Megan was afraid; she had always been afraid of thunder and lightning. That was the reason why I loved it so, because I got to see Megan scared and could feel for once as if I were the big sister.

Joey and I stared out the window into the dark to catch the next brilliant, jagged flash that would write its way across the sky. Megan sat with her crocheting. Each time the room lit up, she dropped it in her lap so she could cover her ears before the crack of thunder. Mom was darning the heels of our socks. It was past our bedtime but she hadn't noticed.

"Joey, where's your other brown sock like this?"

"I don't know."

"Well, if you lost it, I'm wasting my time doing this one." She said it matter-of-fact, not cross.

"Why do you do it anyway?" I asked.

"Because you kids wear them out so fast."

"Well, I hate the lump it makes in my shoe," I said.

"Too bad, dear. We can't afford to get you new ones all the time." She said "we" and that reminded me that Dad wasn't home yet but in some way, it seemed more right than wrong. It seemed as if she'd gotten used to the fact that he hadn't come home for dinner and it was all right. We were just as much a family without him.

She let us make hot chocolate before we went to bed and, for once, all three of us made it without getting into a fight.

Upstairs, Megan and I lay in bed and made places for ourselves in the eerie dark with our soft voices. "What if lightning struck that old tree out there?" she asked me. "It would come right into our room."

"Don't worry," I said. "It's more in line with my bed than yours. Nothing's going to happen. That old tree's been out there for years. That's how it got so old." I tried to get the feeling of being scared. She was right about the tree, it was bound to get struck someday, but the idea of it crashing into our room excited me. It would be a stupendous event, I thought. It would change our lives. They'd have to come with a crane to get it out and Megan and I would have to sleep somewhere else. I was just thinking about lying and telling Megan that I was scared, too, so she could have her proper position back, when Mom started playing the piano.

Mother didn't play the piano often because she thought nobody had any real appreciation of it. Dad had no ear at all for music and the rest of us took our lessons and hated to practice. Mom taught most of our friends but we had to go all the way to West Otis to Mrs. Mooney because we were too sensitive, Mom said. It was true that everytime she tried to correct me, I ended up crying. Secretly, I believed that Mom was a great pianist. At a party she could sit down and play, by ear, anything that was requested. How anyone could do that, chords and all, I found astonishing. When she played for herself, it was from the old music she kept in the piano bench, sheets mended with Scotch tape that had turned yellower than the pages themselves. So worn. That music must have descended from a time when Scotch tape hadn't been invented. Or maybe it was so tattered because she practiced it over and over again, back when she was young, and made that quick reach to turn the page without missing a note. She had old photographs of herself back in Washington Heights, sitting at the piano with Stanley, her long, brown hair flowing down her back. She told us he was the only other man in her life that she'd seriously considered marrying. Still single, Stanley was now a famous pianist, at least famous in New York, and sent her a Christmas card every year to keep her informed of his career. He was a wonderful man, she said, and they'd played for each other for hours. I'd often look at those pictures and wonder what it would be like if Stanley was our father. He was very thin and looked like a rich man to me.

Megan got up and opened the register a crack so we could hear better. The living room was right under our room. Then she crawled back in bed and curled up. The music put her to sleep even though thunder was still crashing outside. As soon as I knew she was asleep, I lost my reckless nerve about the storm. I didn't know the music but I thought I'd concentrate real hard on memorizing it and in the morning I'd ask Mom what it had been. Beethoven was her favorite. It seemed to build and crash while outside the sky cracked open, the timing off, splitting my concentration. Light flashed in the room, aimed at me, attracted to me; then just as fast it was gone. I moved the metal alarm clock down on the floor, over toward Megan's bed. I thought of Ernie, the boy in my class who'd been struck when he was helping his father put the lightning rod on their barn. Was it hundreds or thousands of volts they'd said went through him? Jerking him right out of his shoes so that when he landed down by the roof gutter his shoes were still standing in the place he'd been, all neatly tied and everything. He had a jumpy foot to this day. It was a sort of twitching of the nerves that looked as if the electricity was still trying to get out of him. The thought came to me then that perhaps the American Legion bar had been struck by lightning and instead of dreading each minute that went by and calculating how drunk Dad must be getting, we should be worried about him.

I hadn't yet gotten myself worked up into a good worry when I heard the screen door. Mother must have been too absorbed in her playing because she would've stopped if she had heard him. I heard him stomp through the front hall and he must've been in the doorway when he started bellowing at her, "For God's sake, what are you doing playing that damn thing at this hour? You'll wake the kids." There was an ugly snarl in his voice and the conviction that Mom was the stupidest person in the world. I could have guessed what he looked like, but no, I had to see, I had to make sure. I found myself sliding out of bed, glancing at the sleeping hump that was Megan, and then, like a guerilla warrior, I slithered over to the register on my belly and opened the slats all the way so that the living room was exposed like a stage. I did it without fear of being caught, without the caution Megan and I had used when we did it on Christmas Eve to watch our bicycles being assembled. I did it as though I were a practiced criminal.

He was ugly. His face was red and nasty. I expected he might, any minute, spit on the carpet, which was clean, unspotted, unlike the one in the sitting room where we played. We weren't allowed in the living room except to practice the piano. Dad never went in there either, unless they had guests, so it was strange to see him standing there, swaying as though the storm winds were blowing inside the house. His shirt was half in and half out of his dirty, grey work pants. Mother sat on the piano bench, her straight back to him but her head turned around so she could see him. She crossed her arms on her chest and said, "You're a fine one to be worrying about the kids." I could feel her bristle. I felt it because the same thing happened to me. I didn't move but my body got rigid, stiffened against the hard boards of the floor. She said it very casually but I knew what she meant, knew she was saying that she couldn't trust him to go to town alone and what was she supposed to tell us kids when he didn't come home for dinner and how could she go on facing the neighbors when she never knew what he was doing down there at that bar.

Then he started spitting words at her, saying something about how she thought she was superior because she could play the piano. His mouth hung open, even after he had finished hollering at her back. He took a couple of steps forward, staggered, and then fell heavily into the big arm chair that mother had just finished upholstering. He looked down and his shoulders drooped and I thought he would fall asleep right then and there.

Mother sidled to the end of the piano bench farthest from him and stood up and continued sidling as though she could sneak out of the room. It was our way. You convince yourself he is really blind and only talking to himself. You think if you're quiet about the way you exit, he'll never know.

But she didn't get away. She got about halfway to the door and he called her over and that's when it happened, something horrible that I didn't understand. It wasn't sex. I'd just learned from Megan what she had learned from Donnie, next door, about sex. The man peed into the woman, into her private part. I didn't know what he was doing, only that he made her come over to the side of his chair and stand there like an obedient child and then he pulled her skirt up at the sides and tucked it into her waist band so that it hung scalloped and then he pulled her panties down until they were around her ankles. Somehow he had a hold of her because every time she tried to move away, he pulled her back and hollered at her— "Stand still." Maybe I closed my eyes after that. I don't know. I just wanted her to get away from him, and finally I saw her run into the dining room.

I crawled back into bed, shivering uncontrollably, my teeth chattering so loudly I was sure they'd wake Megan. I held the blankets tightly with my fists over my head and even though my eyes were closed, I felt as if my eyeballs were popping out. I started breathing fast and I wondered if it were possible that I hadn't breathed the whole time I'd been down there on the floor.

It couldn't have been more than one or two minutes later—I had gotten myself calmed down a little and was trying to pretend it had only been a bad nightmare—when the scream came. It was Mother. It pierced through my blankets. It had to be her. It sounded as though she were splitting in two. I had never heard her scream before. I couldn't tell whether it was going on and on, or if it was just echoing in my ears. It was the only sound. The rain had stopped. Then Megan was shaking and poking at the lump of me under the blankets. "Francie, Francie, something happened." She commanded me, "Come out. You have to come with me," and I made the mistake of letting go of the blanket to put my hands over my ears and she yanked it back. She pulled me by the hand until my feet were on the floor and then she dragged me down the hall and down the stairs.

Mom and Dad were lying on the floor in the hallway between the dining room and the kitchen. He was lying half on his side and half on his stomach, completely limp. Mother was holding him around the chest with one arm, pushing her bosom into him, where the blood was. She had her eyes squeezed tightly closed, she didn't even know we were there, and she was murmuring to him, "I'll fix you up, Jack. It's going to be all right. I didn't mean it. I love you. I'll fix you up." I couldn't keep myself from staring at them. Joey was standing behind me and I heard his breath come out in a whoosh and then he said, "Jesus Christ," which is what Dad always said either after he had hammered his finger or when he was very surprised, not sure he believed something. Megan stood next to me with her hands clasped in front of her. Stiff, frozen, she stared into the kitchen. The most horrifying thing was his cheek, the way the floor pressed against it, flattening it uncomfortably, making it look the way your nose does from the other side of the pane when you press it against a window. I had seen it like that once before when he had put his head directly down on the table and passed out. His eyes weren't completely closed but I couldn't see into them. I stepped into the small space behind his back and bent over. "Daddy, Daddy, please wake up," I whispered. I stroked his hair. It felt normal but he didn't move. Mother opened her eyes then and saw me and her mouth opened and I thought she was going to scream again but she only worked it back and forth and nothing came out. When she moved back from him a little, I saw blood spurting from his chest. Red, red, live blood, pumping out, waterfalling off his grey shirt. A pool of it on the floor between them and also there, on the floor, was our butcher knife, a watery film of blood hiding the shiny metal. I stepped over his head then and ran to the bathroom and threw up, kneeling on the floor by the toilet, feeling that I would faint except for the horrible taste in my mouth that made me keep spitting and gagging, clenching the toilet with both hands, my fists clamped to it so tight that my knuckles were almost porcelain white. I wanted so badly for Mom to come in and stroke my forehead, pushing back the damp hair, as she usually did when I was sick to my stomach. I listened for her but I only heard the Carters. Ethel and Charlie from across the road. They must've heard the scream. Charlie was yelling at Ethel that Dad was bleeding to death. "Get something to stop the bleeding. I'll call an ambulance."

I was alone. No one even wondered where I was. I didn't want to go back out there, but I couldn't stand being so alone.

Ethel was on her knees, shoving all the towels from the linen closet up into his chest. Mother was gone from her place beside him. He looked smaller than I'd always thought him to be, but very heavy, like the fox carcass in the dream. I had to step over his head again to get back in the other room and as I did, I said, "Hello, Ethel," just as if it were an ordinary day, as if she were dressed in her lovely, tailored clothes instead of her bathrobe, as if she were doing us a little favor like examining the new kittens to tell us whether they were male or female.

Then I saw Mother sitting in the far corner of the dining room, on the floor. She didn't look like my mother. She looked like an orphan who didn't belong in our house. Her skirt was draped across her lap and she had vomited into it. Her eyes were blank, staring at me but not understanding it was me. I moved away, out of her line of vision and stumbled into Joey. My arms felt so useless, hanging from my body with nothing to do and my legs, too, because I didn't know where to go, where to stand. Joey was sobbing quietly, so I hugged him tight and told him to close his eyes and then I started to cry too. We stayed, rocking and swaying together, until we heard the sirens and Ethel told Charlie, "Take the children out. Take the children over to our house. I'll stay. I'll ride in to the hospital with Laura."

"Laura, can you get up?" she said. I watched Mother out of the corner of my eye. She seemed not to hear. She made no effort though from time to time her arms jerked as though she'd been struck by lightning. She reminded me of the chickens, the way their bodies twitched and jumped after Dad had chopped off their heads for Sunday dinner. Over in the Carter's driveway, we watched the disaster flicker of the red lights on the ambulance. Charlie kept telling us we should go in the house, but we held back. We watched them bring the two stretchers down the porch stairs. The sheet was pulled up all the way, over Dad's head.

FIVE

Ethel used to come walking across the side yard, her stride long and leisurely, her golden collie at her side. She'd be on her way in to have coffee with Mom but if I was on the swing, she always stopped and pulled me all the way back, all the way up to her full height, so that the top of my head got tickled by the leaves, and then saying, "Hold tight now," she'd let loose and my stomach would flip once. The dog, Bessie, would run beside me, back and forth, back and forth, her path getting shorter and shorter as the swing lost momentum.

We stayed at Ethel's house for the three days while Mom was in the hospital. She went to see her the first morning and came home with a report. "She is in shock," she told us. "She needs some rest and then she'll be okay. They're taking good care of her."

I went upstairs to the attic bedroom. It was my favorite room in the Carter's house and I'd often wished I could sleep there instead of my own room across the street. The ceiling sloped right down to the beds on either side of the dormer window. I lay on my back and stared at the ceiling and tried to imagine what shock looked like. I couldn't get away from the idea of electricity and the picture I formed had thunderbolts dancing zigzags inside Mom, sizzling around the roots of her hairs making them stand straight up and bulging her eyes out of their sockets. But I couldn't imagine her lying in a bed that way. Not at all. I couldn't imagine someone taking care of her. Not Mom. Every morning of my life she'd been down in the kitchen cracking the eggs, one-handed, into the frying pan. Now she was resting all day long, in shock. I wondered if they had tied her hands down to the sides of the bed.

I was sitting in the window seat when the sheriff's car drove into our driveway. Bessie was barking at him from the edge of the yard. Ethel told her to stay as she crossed the road and went over and took the sheriff into our house. Bessie stayed and cried a sing-song moan until Ethel was out of sight.

The sheriff was one of those people everybody knew, at least all the men did. I didn't know how Dad had gotten to know him, but I remembered him going up to the sheriff and shaking his hand at the last county fair. Perhaps he was one of those men who sat down there at the American Legion bar. Seeing him clomp up our porch steps in his boots made me remember the way that we'd left the house; the blood must still be there. It was the first time I realized that what had happened might be a crime, that it didn't just have to do with our family. My vision of Mother with her hands tied down to the bed in the hospital turned into Mother with her hands tied to bars. I swallowed hard around a lump of self pity, thinking about being an orphan, imagining myself comparing notes with the other kids in an orphan school. No, Mom would explain. It was self-defense. She'd explain that he'd forced her, done something to her that she couldn't stand.

I had no idea how long I'd been staring through the window when Ethel came back out, carrying a bag filled with clean clothes for us, and the sheriff left. Maybe I was in shock, too. I only went down to the kitchen when she called for all of us.

We sat at the round table in the middle of the room and she poured us milk in juice glasses from a quart bottle that looked like a toy because we were used to gallons. Ethel and Charlie didn't have any children, only Bessie and the cats. She put the cookie jar in the center, took the lid off and said,

"Help yourselves." We all sat, munching big sugar cookies, trying to be polite and not to leave too many crumbs.

"You must've seen the sheriff," she said.

"What was he doing?" Joey asked.

"He has to write up an investigation."

"Oh," Megan said, as if that was an every day event and she understood everything about it.

"Are we going to be questioned?" Joey asked, a routine question on the outlaw radio programs that normally provided the thrills in our lives.

"I don't think that will be necessary," Ethel said and then proceeded to question us. She wanted to know if Dad had been home for dinner and we told her no, he hadn't been home all night. If only she'd questioned us separately maybe I could have told her what I saw, but we all sat there together and I kept eating sugar cookies while Megan and Joey explained that he must've been at the American Legion getting drunk. Then Ethel said that she and the sheriff had figured out what happened. That they'd noticed the grate on the floor in the hallway and it all fit together. Dad must've tripped and fallen on the knife. He'd been drunk and naturally not walking too steady and possibly he hadn't even realized that she'd been holding the knife.

Maybe. Maybe that's what happened. At least it gave me a start in seeing something: I saw Dad in the hallway, looming large, a monstrous form, and Mom, her brittle, stiff back holding her in place like a cat who has turned fierce foe, preparing to spit and scratch. Still, I couldn't imagine the actual moment of them coming together, the moment of contact. And I couldn't imagine him tripping on that grate we'd all been stepping across for years.

I kept waiting for Ethel to say more but she was finished, she was thinking to herself, drinking her coffee and keeping an eye on us. Ethel with her strong, handsome face, with her eyes that looked right into yours, I couldn't believe she was satisfied that they'd figured it out just like that. I would wager a bet that she had much more the detective mind than the sheriff, having overheard many of her conversations with Mother.

I remembered the day I'd been down on the kitchen floor drawing a picture of a tall, stately woman and Ethel had said to Mom, "You know, Francie is very clever and determined and she'll use those traits to get somewhere." She had no way of knowing that my picture was of her. She went on to tell Mom how she thought Megan was very sociable and never afraid of people and Megan would go places too. "Yes, they're good kids," Mom had said. I don't think she believed Ethel. She didn't seem to think we were capable of individuality, but rather conceived of us as extensions of herself, who would one day, almost magically, take on sets of traits which would distinguish us, one from the other. She treated our childhood traits much as deciduous teeth. They would all fall out and be replaced with new ones.

The time when all the parents were down on Miss Barnes for making Peter get up in front of the fifth grade class and tell how cows were artificially inseminated, Ethel was the only one who said she didn't think it was so horrible. She was just curious to know exactly how Peter had explained it, and also wondered what it might be like to live all alone up on that hill like Miss Barnes. Ethel was always wanting to know what went on behind the doors of people's houses but not in a gossipy way; she *really* wanted to know,

"You might feel differently if you had kids," Mom had said to her.

"I might," she admitted, "but I don't think so."

She got up and put the glasses in the sink. Then she stood behind me and cupped her hands around my shoulders. "You children are being very courageous," she said. "Whenever you feel like talking about anything, I'll be here. I'll be here all the time and if I have to go out, Charlie will be here. I want you to come to me when you want to talk." I wanted to talk but

I couldn't say anything. Mostly I just wanted her to keep her hands on my shoulders.

I would have spent the next three days in the attic bedroom if Ethel hadn't kept bringing us down to talk. She talked to us all the time so that staying with her got to be almost like a reward for having lost our parents, or at least Dad. She talked about the accident and how terrible we must feel, and about Dad and how much she had always liked him despite his stubborn ways, and she asked us questions about every conceivable thing, listening as if she really wanted to hear as we droned out the answers. What did we feel like doing after lunch? Did we sleep all right in her house? Had we had any nightmares? What did we think of Miss Gildersleeve, the second grade teacher who made you slap the back of your own hand with a ruler if you got caught talking? Our grandparents were coming up for the funeral. What did we think about that? Did we like them? Until that moment, we had never conceived the idea of not liking them.

"Yes," I said. "They're always nice to us. And when they come to visit we have tea at four o'clock because that's their custom. When we were small, Grandma Gerty used to pretend she could read our fortunes from the tea leaves," I told her.

"And now you don't believe in that?" Ethel asked.

"No, I don't think so. The fortunes were always too much alike."

"Does she sing to you?" Ethel asked.

"Yes."

"She has a beautiful voice," Ethel said.

"Yeah, but she sings that icky music," Joey said.

If he hadn't said that, I would've told Ethel about how her singing made my spine tingle.

"If I had known you were tea drinkers, I would've served you tea instead of milk," she said. "Tomorrow we'll have tea."

But the next day was the funeral. Mother got out of the hospital and went home to dress and then came over to get us, and I couldn't look at her except out of the corner of my eye. She didn't look like she was in shock anymore. She kept at a distance and asked about the things we'd been doing, as though she'd been away on a vacation but had come back exhausted instead of rested. I knew from the way she came around inspecting us to see if we were properly dressed for the funeral that we were all going to put on a show and that I wasn't going to be able to ask her what had happened in the living room. I had tried a couple of times to tell Ethel but I hadn't been able to get it out. For one thing, I worried that she might say—"For God's sakes, why didn't you tell me that before"—or even—"Why didn't you do something? You might've stopped them." What worried me even more was that it seemed such a private thing to tell and it didn't seem fair to Mother. I felt that telling would somehow mean I was giving her up and taking Ethel as my mother. Seeing Mom again, and feeling the place where she had gouged my skull with the bobby pin so as to be sure that my hat would stay on properly, I wished I had told.

I was relieved to find out that Grandma Gerty and Pappy were meeting us at the church, that we didn't have to go over to the house, because no one had ever mentioned cleaning up the blood and I couldn't help wondering with horror if it was still there. I guessed that someone must have done it but I couldn't imagine who or how they did it or what they did with the rags afterwards.

I tried to listen to what the priest was saying, but not a word caught. On my left, Aunt May was fully occupied with her rosary, her lips moving silently, rapidly. I couldn't keep track of what bead I was on. Besides, I had no desire for God or Jesus or Mary or any of them to be near me. I wanted to concentrate on my father, and it seemed that as long as his casket was there in front of us, he wasn't gone yet. I remembered all of his funny riddles and I almost laughed out loud right there in the church, but I remembered we were in public and we were doing the show of the proper family. I got this terrible desire to ask him about King, our favorite dog, about why he had lied to us and told us that King must've just run off and got lost because he was so old. I had found his grave in the woods a few months later. It was two pieces of wood nailed together to make a cross and KING was carved in the top board. I wanted to ask him why he had done that. I wanted to ask him even though he couldn't answer, but the priest was walking around the casket, sprinkling it with holy water.

The worst moment for me was when they lowered him into the hole in the ground and the heavy box with all his dead-weight in it sounded with a thud when it hit the earth. It was the most final sound I had ever heard. Besides hearing the actual sound with my ears, I felt it, the jarring of the earth through my feet. That was it then. He was gone and he would not come back. I had always thought King would come running into the yard some day, until I had found the grave.

After that thud, nothing was distinct. My eyes were blurred with tears and I couldn't concentrate on figuring anything out. A lot of people came back to the house and sat around the table, which was made enormous by the addition of two leaves. It didn't look right. It looked like a holiday. Someone must've cooked because the table was piled with food and my aunt kept saying I should eat, but my stomach felt as if it had flipped upside down. Mom had a cloth napkin squeezed in her hand and once in a while she pressed it against one eye, then the other, while Aunt May went on about Granny's funeral, about how if Joe, Jr. and Nell had managed to drive up to Pennsylvania on the icy roads for Granny, there was no excuse for their not having come just this couple hours further to upstate New York, before the first snow and all.

I was out on the porch when Mr. Drake from the grocery store went home. He came up and said in his most formal voice, "An awful accident, I'm sorry." He shook his head as if he were shaking the creeps away and I didn't know what to say, but I figured I was supposed to say something, so I said, "Thank you."

The whole day no one fell apart. "I'm very proud of you kids. Let's get up to bed now," Mom said when everyone was gone.

The chickens got put in crates and carted off, clucking at the disturbance. I, personally, didn't mind seeing them go. I figured the school nurse would hear of it and stop picking us out with the other farmer kids as prime suspects for head-lice.

Mom never explained anything. She got a job keeping the books down at the feed store. She told us she didn't want us to be disturbed by the fact that she had to go through a court procedure.

"Why?" we asked, not sure if we meant why did she have to go through it or why shouldn't we be disturbed.

"A formality," she said.

I looked the word up in a dictionary and found out it meant what I thought it meant—nothing. She doled out information as sparsely as she served her own plate at the table. She ate the chicken wings and looked frail, her cheeks hollow, her sweater sagging between her shoulder blades. Megan, Joey and I didn't fight much and the lid stayed down over the piano keys, except when we had to practice.

Some days when I got home from school, Ethel would call from her front door and invite me in for tea. That's where I saw the story in the *Oswego Star*, down in the right hand corner on the front page.

MRS. KELLY GIVEN SUSPENDED SENTENCE

Mrs. Kelly, originally charged with first degree murder, pleaded guilty to the lesser charge of manslaughter and was sentenced yesterday by Judge Hartman to five years imprisonment. The sentence was immediately suspended.

Mrs. Kelly, mother of three, was accused in the death of her husband, Jack Kelly, who was declared dead on arrival, November 17th, at Oswego County

Hospital, of stab wounds. Mrs. Kelly's attorney requested the mercy of the court in considering both her testimony regarding the incident (Mrs. Kelly testified that she was in a state of fear of her drunken husband and had no recollection of picking up a knife and that she had never intended to harm him) and her upstanding reputation in the community. Mrs. Kelly is a past president of the Otis Central School P.T.A. Her attorney described the stabbing as an unfortunate accident in which Mr. Kelly tripped at the wrong moment. He cited the testimony of neighbors who attested to the fact that Mrs. Kelly had never been known to have malicious intent toward anyone.

Ethel had gone to get something while the water was on. I turned the paper back over. She came in with the scissors and I knew I was going to cry if she asked me how I was, but she didn't. She clipped back some of the plants in the window.

"I promised your mother some cuttings," she said. She put them in a jelly glass and placed it beside me so I could remember to take it home. The tea was steeping in the pot.

"How's school?"

"Okay."

"What's on your mind?" she asked.

I tried to get bravery and maturity into my voice. "I read the thing in the paper . . . about court."

"Oh." We sat silently for a minute. "I went to get the scissors because I wanted to clip it," she said. "Then I remembered about the cuttings."

"What does it mean?" By the time I got the question out, my lips were jerking and my eyes were burning. Ethel came around behind my chair and stood and turned my head sideways. Holding her hand against my cheek, she pressed me against her stomach. I could feel my hot tears running onto her cool hand. "It's okay," she said. "It means everything's going to be okay. Your mother had to plead guilty. That was just a technicality, the best way for the lawyer to be sure she'd be given a suspended sentence."

"What's a suspended sentence?"

"It's just a way of sentencing someone, because a guilty plea means you have to be sentenced, then removing it immediately. You see?"

"Not really."

"Don't try to understand the legal system, dear. It doesn't even make much sense to me. Charlie knew the judge and he knew it had to be done this way, that's all. What's important is that it's all over and your mother's finished with it and she's doing fine."

But had she told? Had Ethel been there when she testified? Did she tell what Daddy had done to her? Did everybody know? Why couldn't I get these questions to just go away?

Ethel brought me a tissue to blow my nose and wipe my eyes and we drank our tea in silence. The newspaper told what happened. There it was in print. Ethel clipped it out and stuck it inside the flap of the book she was reading.

I went home and put the cuttings on the kitchen sink. Mom was still at work. I went out to the back yard and sat with my back pressed hard against the bark of one of the big trees. The ground was frozen and snow flurries were coming down, the first of the winter. I wondered if I had gotten all mixed up about what I had seen, if Dad really had grabbed Mom and made her stay there by the chair, if that could be a normal thing for a man to do to his wife.

I'd never let anyone do it to me, I knew that much. I was getting colder and colder. I thought about lying flat out on the ground and letting the snow cover me. You always heard about people getting lost and freezing to death while they were trying to climb a mountain. How ridiculous it would be to hear about a twelve-year-old girl getting lost in her own back yard, lying stiff, buried, until the snow melted in the spring.

SIX

I rang Lisa's buzzer and she said she'd be right down. Arthur must've been home. I'd met him once at the tail end of a group meeting when I'd hung around after the others had left. "Sorry," he'd said, "I didn't mean to interrupt anything."

"Oh, we're finished," I'd said, feeling the intruder. You can have her back now.

Lisa came through the door, gave me a quick, firm hug and brushed my cheek with her lips. "Where to?"

"I don't know but we might as well walk toward the Village while we're deciding."

I could feel a springiness in my body when I walked with her, almost a memory of myself before Dad's death, of running the fields, racing Debbie, racing Joey, racing Zeke. Running, but not at the end of the whip.

We decided on The Bellybutton for a light snack because it was always fairly quiet there. It was quiet because it was so narrow, an alley restaurant. We sat at the far end, face to face.

"How was work?" Lisa asked.

"Hard. A woman died. . . she didn't actually but it looked like she did. . . . I thought she had died in my arms."

"Sounds gruesome."

"Not really. It did shake me up though."

"I would imagine."

"About myself. I'm not sure what it means." I didn't say more. I didn't know what to say.

"I don't understand," she said after a minute of silence.

"This woman. . . she woke up the dead in me. I've been walking around shaking ever since."

Tears were rising behind my eyes. I didn't want to cry in The Bellybutton. Lisa watched me so closely I felt as if she could see me from inside. "Do you want to talk more about it?" she asked.

"Not now," I said. "What's happening with you?"

"Same," she said, "Same problem, same solution, same pain, same place. Maybe not the same place. I've looked through the *Voice* ads. And the pain moves too." The tears came to her eyes but she didn't stop talking. "It's going to be very hard," she said. "I've never in my life lived alone. I'm not equipped for it. Arthur was my brother."

Arthur was her husband. She was an only child who had married him when they were both seventeen. Lisa's face was heart shaped, her cheeks full. Tears perched on her cheek bones, quivered, then ran. The waitress came. "Shall we have her come back later?" I asked.

"No, let's order," she said. "I'll have a Bellybutton omelet."

"Cheeseburger, medium," I said, without taking my eyes from her tears.

"There are ways in which I still love him," she said.

I didn't admit it, but at least I didn't have that problem with Ben. Lisa cried all the way through dinner, not in a stream but with those same pairs of tears which would perch, then run. She seemed almost unaware of the wetness of her cheeks. I heard her words and stored them to go over later. I could not concentrate on anything but my intense urge to reach across the table and touch her cheek with the back of my hand, touch the wet, beautiful skin of her face. She was the one who broke the spell, taking both hands at once and briskly pushing aside the wet as if she'd just come up from an underwater swim, saying, "My God, I'm a mess. I wish I had your control."

I was sorry I had not figured out a way to touch her before she'd done the job, and so quick and without warning. "Don't wish it," I said. "I like you better the way you are."

Girls' night at the Sunday evening youth meeting—we handed in anonymous questions for the priest to answer. I'd gotten the idea for my question after confession the day before, a confession it had taken me weeks to work up the courage for. Stealing my mother's cigarettes, one from each pack she opened, and confessing only the little stuff week to week—"I forgot to say my morning and evening prayers twice." Walking away from the altar on Sundays till the count was up to thirty-nine and I knew the sticky host was going to choke me, so I looked it up in the book and found out the thing to do was to repeat all my bad confessions.

The slat clapped open and my heart jumped in the dark. "I have stolen thirty-nine times. All my confessions for the past four months have been bad ones," I said.

I gulped, preparing for the recitation of my lengthy list and he interrupted me, "What did you steal?"

"My mother's cigarettes."

Because of the noise of my breath and the commotion the list was making in my brain, I couldn't be sure if the priest had chuckled. "Well, dear, your past confessions will stand," he said. "That is a venial sin and you don't have to confess venial sins, though it's best to do so."

I wanted to scream. Why didn't they put that in the book? After all my sweat. Thou Shalt Not Steal. I thought it was mortal no matter how you did it.

And immediately I'd started thinking, "That means there must be variations for all the ten commandments."

There were three rows of thirteen to fifteen-year-olds and I sat in the middle of the middle row. He read off the questions, formulating answers as he went along. "What is the difference between necking and petting? What is French kissing?

Is it a sin? Why?" He had a slight, palsy shake to his hands. "Is there such a thing as a murder that isn't a mortal sin? For instance, is manslaughter a venial sin?"

"No," he said, solemnly. "All murders are mortal sins. Thou Shalt Not Kill. One of the ten commandments." He had looked at me when he said it. I was sure he knew it was my question. Yes, he knew and all the girls knew, too. I tried to keep the rush of blood down, out of my face, to concentrate on French kissing. Thou Shalt Not Steal. Why was that different? It had been stupid, really stupid of me to have thought my question would mix in with all the others. I sat in shame, begging my tear ducts to stay closed, while he answered the rest of the questions, giving us guidance on how to eliminate sexual exploration from our lives. Then he left and the girls quickly formed clusters, snickered and compared Father O'Leary's definition of French kissing with their own. I wanted to hear. I wanted to know, just as much as anyone else, all there was to know about French kissing, but I couldn't stay. I wished I could crawl, head-first, inside my own skin. No one noticed when I slipped out and walked home.

Once in, there was no slipping out of a consciousness raising group, nor could I simply slip away from Ben. Nor could I go on moving from one to the other, so frankly incompatible were they. Yet I had been invited to the group by a woman who was a friend of Ben's, who thought Ben a feminist, who didn't know (because I didn't tell her) that the laundry bag had been waiting by the door for days because it was his turn, because he needed time to overcome his domestic resistance, because he knew I would probably do it myself when my underwear ran out before his.

Lisa had joined a couple of weeks after me. She had bounced in, engaged us all with her large, brown eyes and articulated, without the need to stammer or flounder, how avidly she was prepared to pursue her liberation. She had summarized her life in the equivalent of a page, a page organized to create the impression that nothing was left out. Having left out large gaps of my own life in my description of myself, I became an immediate admirer. Since I had been spending more time with her outside the group, I had found out some of the things she did leave out. She had gone off to Europe, had an affair, come home with a report for her husband and demanded the freedom to have variety in her life. Now, *he* was having an affair, telling her, and demanding reciprocity.

"I must have the freedom to explore the areas of my life that have been subdued," she'd told the group.

"I never thought he'd let someone else be important," she'd told me over her Bellybutton omelet. This was my first clue that the venial sins were often being left out during the confessional ritual of consciousness raising.

Still, I felt more comfortable when I plopped down there on Tally's rug in the loose circle than I'd ever felt with any group before. In spite of the lies or omissions, we were building a pyramid of truth in the center of our circle. Each story told became another block and each block was there for us all. Week after week I would go home from these meetings, provoked to the point of insomnia, lie next to snoring Ben and rerun the dialogue of the meeting until I had it memorized.

I suffered terrible temptations to tell my Mother's story, not just the stabbing but the part that preceded it, the part I had failed to tell Ethel. These women were the first I had ever known who talked about rape with anger, who talked about women without sandwiching men in between, who were learning to disregard all they had learned about being the protectors of men. When I was with them I was almost sure that I could remember what my eyes had seen through the register; the rest of the time a fog seemed to sit on my memory, dimming any possibility of clarity, as it had through all the years since the accident up to then.

Andrea's face was cherubic. In another generation she might have been a nun. Now she was a lesbian who did a lot of meditating. Tally was also a lesbian. She had tufts of silky, black, underarm hair which she displayed in warm weather.

She had two grown children and was almost my mother's age. I had difficulty believing in her age, yet I believed that she, of all the women, was the most truthful. Margo was tall and graceful and referred to herself as the "odd one out." Joan was chubby and had a tendency to smile too much. Lisa sat with her back very erect as if she had taken on a strict discipline.

I was edgy about groups, edgy about the morning incident with Gwyn. And I had sworn years ago in my anguish over Father O'Leary's response never to put myself up for that kind of scrutiny again. Margo could call herself the "odd one out." I would run the tail on the end of the whip until I beat it.

We started around the circle on the subject of the violence in our lives. Margo talked about karate, her thrill with the utterances that went with a blow, and her preparation for the moment which would come in the future when she would strike. I listened. I tried to let myself go completely to the listening but couldn't. What was I going to say about violence in my life? I had forgotten about the subject which we had selected the week before. I had meant to plan what I would say.

Margo had finished and Lisa was describing the knockdown-drag-out fights she'd often had with Arthur. "After I throw all the books on the bookshelf at him and then attack him with my fingernails, he overpowers me, pins my arms up against the wall. . . . Okay," she said, "now don't ask me how but inevitably we end up in bed having a terrific fuck. Later I feel dirty. I'm beginning to realize that lashing out isn't the thing I need to improve. I've always done that well." She said she'd been brought up on it and it disgusted her the way her parents had nourished each other through a lifetime by flashing their shiny, gritted teeth and grabbing the heaviest, handiest, threatening object and flinging their sharp comments, designed to slice you to the bone.

It was my turn. I had gotten lost in her story and still hadn't figured out what to say. Her words rang in the silence while all eyes moved to me. I opened and closed my mouth a few times but nothing came out. I felt sure that I looked like a fish with my mouth moving that way. Still, they kept their eyes on me and no one interrupted the silence. A large ball swelled in my throat and ached. I didn't think I could talk around it. They didn't know Ben. They only knew the false front of what I had told them about him. Finally, that didn't matter. "I'm leaving Ben," I said. The statement erupted into a sobbing laugh.

"Why?" Joan asked.

"Because I've developed an aversion to him," I said. They laughed. Tears broke and came streaming down my cheeks then, and the lump was melting, letting me swallow again.

"What do you mean by an aversion?" Tally asked.

"I don't know. That just seems like what it is." I laughed then with all of them, the laughter coming from release, as if, having lived my whole life with suspenders always pulling my pants too tight up into my crotch, I had made one grand stretch which popped them off. I laughed in such a way that my face felt contorted. Finally I became silent, and then could speak again.

"It's not that I'm scared of being without him. Not at all. I look forward to that. It's just that I have to tell him I'm leaving and I know he'll try to turn my words around. It's impossible to talk to him. All I want to do is hit him."

"Maybe you should," Tally said.

"No," I said. "No, I couldn't. I need to be able to tell him. I need to be able to use words."

Lisa nodded, understanding. I felt bare in the presence of their eyes but I also felt the harmony of the feelings of the room. The way these women held silence while I searched for my next thought, the way they waited with me until it emerged, gave me a focus that made it possible to see that it was within my rights simply to leave Ben because I wanted to, because I wanted something more for my life. I didn't have to know what.

SEVEN

Ben was stretched out on the couch, watching Dick Cavett. Every bourgeois bone in his body had found a resting place in the luxurious nap, in the heavy stuffing that displaced the perfect amount just as the sofa's price had promised. It was obvious that he'd slept off his afternoon suspicions. He looked like a man whose life was in order. I walked through the living room on the edge of paranoia, fearing my body would give away my intentions before I got my mouth open. My lips felt rigid and dry and I was sure I looked unnatural.

"Hi. How are you?" he said, his tone familiar.

Dummy, what are you doing hanging up your coat? You're leaving, I said to myself. I stepped into the bathroom and checked my look in the mirror. Not bad. I looked much more like myself than I felt.

"Come here." He had said it casually enough but I panicked. I didn't want to go near him; he was onto me.

"Why?"

"What do you mean, why? I just wanted to kiss you."

"Can I turn the T.V. off? I have to talk to you."

"Of course." He caught the tension in my voice and came to a semi-sitting position. I cut Dick Cavett in the middle of a joke. Instant silence. "Start right away," I told myself, "before he does."

"It's no good," I said. "No good for me anyway, I'm leaving. I have to." I paced the room. I had a strange feeling that as long as I remained standing I could keep control, I had the stage. I think it must have been the first time in my life I'd taken a serious stand without sitting down. I'd always had the feeling that I had to sit to protect my internal organs, to shield them by my posture, to avoid the roller-coaster fear of my stomach dropping all the way to the floor.

Ben wasn't responding, only staring at me, his recessed eyes popping to attention. He followed my paces with an incredulous expression on his face. It wasn't fair to come out with it like this, no warning. What had happened to my Monday, Tuesday, Wednesday plan which had taken into account his need for a gradual awakening?

The silence nagged at the seams of my armor. I went to the other end of the couch and sat down. It was either that or go to the closet and take out my coat. He got up and took the stage. "Well, is that all I get? After living with you for almost two years, you suddenly come up with 'I'm leaving' and is that it?"

"A year and a half," I said, relieved to have an objective fact on my side. He was angry and his anger made him seem ugly, ugly and too tall to be human. He belonged in a fairy tale or a cartoon. I felt very small and tired and feeble.

"Do you mind telling me why?" Sneering, as though no one had ever told him the why of anything.

"Please, Ben. This isn't easy for me. Don't treat me that way. I think you know why. I've tried to tell you before. The combination just doesn't work, you and me. You mow me down. I don't survive as myself with you. You know the things, your things that I've succumbed to, your jealousies, your ideas about how I shouldn't talk about relationships I've had in the past. I don't really accept that. I've just pretended to for your sake. I can't live that way and you need someone who can."

"Don't tell me what I need." Then calmly he said, "Did that group of women tell you you should do this?"

I hadn't really been angry till then. I had gotten over

most of my fear once it was out, conclusively, that I was leaving. I had felt a sense of civility when I had sat down. And some relief, as if I had walked across a thin ice pond, treading lightly but steadily, and having reached the other side without sabotaging myself, the only mission I had left was to watch him grasping at the edges of the hole he had fallen through, to watch his long arms extending to reach me though I was obviously far beyond his span. I had felt that my part was over and that I needed only to sit on the spectator couch and pay proper respects by keeping my eyes on him, recording his words and waiting for him to run down with fatigue. But his asking that question, his trying to identify the enemy, his sureness that it had to be someone else putting ideas in my idle little head, his scornful conviction that he need only know who and then he could launch a successful attack, brought the adrenaline rushing into my blood. I was livid. If he had been grasping at the edge of an ice hole, I would have walked over and stomped on his fingers. As it was only a drama of dialogue and posture and invisible visceral spasms, however, I stayed on the couch and felt my temples pulsing and the muscles in the back of my neck drawing tight, and the weight of my head burdening me. My head needed so badly to lie down. I thought of the little hydrocephalic girl I'd seen once while touring an institution for the mentally retarded. The small body with the enormous, beach-ball head, the head so heavy there was no lifting it. She lay in the crib with mirrors strategically placed around her and her eyes followed me around the room, cooly shifting from one mirror to the next.

"No, my group didn't tell me what to do," I said, keeping the mirrors in mind to hold my distance.

"I know we just went through this, but I want to know if it's another man." He proceeded with his usual elaborations on the other man possibilities. The pressure rising in me as if I were in a pressure cooker, cooking fast—rare, medium, well-done—the blood all gone, the flesh sizzling, drying out, dying.

"There is no other man." I screamed it to interrupt him and get his attention. He stopped pacing, shocked at my decibels. I calmed myself to start again. "Look, if you want to talk, you'll just have to talk to me, about me. There's no other man. No one told me to do this. The more I'm with you the more anonymous I've become and I can't stand that part of myself. . . and it seems to me that's the part you love. Your kind of love doesn't seem to have anything to do with me as me, just with me as being here for you."

"That's not true."

"Ben, it doesn't matter if it's true. It's the way I feel. I don't really expect you to agree."

"We've been so good for each other. . . ."

"That's from your side. You don't even consider me capable of deciding for myself whether or not you're good for me." My shoulders were scrunched up around my neck. My pressure-cooked anger came out with the twang of a grievance.

"You're wrong," he said. "I do. I consider you capable of just about anything. You're so damned capable it's ridiculous. It's just that I've been preoccupied. I've been too self-centered," He then repeated almost every dreadful thing that had ever happened to him. I sat, catching only fragments of his sad story, hanging on to my own life. Then he pleaded, "Francie, please, I want you to give it another chance. It can work. I'll make it work. Please." (He'll make it work. He doesn't understand the first thing about twos. Never got past number one, never understood that beyond yourself you have to relinquish control.)

My face felt pasty hard, as if it were a mask. My fingers were ice cold. I hadn't cried a tear through this whole tear-jerker. I concentrated on holding up my heavy head. I felt like an inanimate object. I told him I couldn't feel and I couldn't stand it and I had to get away and find my nerve endings.

He didn't hear me. Refusing to acknowledge the wall surrounding me, he went on poking for holes through which he might elicit my sympathy, until finally I burst at him, "Stop it. Stop trying to make me feel guilty. I didn't cause your life. Leave me alone." I was shaking then.

"I'm going now," I said, standing. "We'll have to work something out about my things. I'll come by and pick them up over the weekend." When he came over to me I realized I'd been waiting for his permission to leave. He held me but I remained rigid as a telephone pole, concentrating on the vertical plane because it seemed the only thing of importance. If I should sway just one degree, the scene would be prolonged. He would swoop in with a whole new set of promises, he would lay bare his needs again, he would find a new slant for them, and I wasn't up to withstanding any of these things. I was dead to him and yet, if he hadn't sensed that and stopped at that point, I think I would have turned on him savagely. Growled and clawed at him or kicked his skinny shin bones and pounded on his chest. I don't know what I would have done.

We stood by the door, he kissing my eyelids, my nose, my cheeks, as if he wanted to leave me soft, but even as he did that, I felt he was trying to take my last softness for himself, confiscating it and leaving me even more rigid. I shivered in my coat. I wished him good luck and happiness through a crack in my mask. He made me promise to reconsider. "Yes, I will," I said, lying.

I was out.

It was three o'clock in the morning. I walked home without worrying about the other people I passed on the street. I knew I was unapproachable. I felt like a mummy who had learned the trick of ambulation long ago in another life and carried on now without sensation. I feared for a second that I had made a wrong turn and was going in the wrong direction though I had walked the same streets for years.

Home, I watched myself in the bathroom mirror. My face. My mask. It was white, still. The eyes were red. The muscles in my cheeks were wadded up, stiff. The numbness was unbearable. I was a freak. Unfeeling, dull, paralyzed. I wondered if the paralysis would be permanent. I was horrified by the prospect, but my mask didn't show horror. It showed a ghost. I had a certain fascination with watching this face. I recalled the woman I'd seen at a masquerade party who had appeared to be dancing with her back to her partner. Then she'd turned and I'd seen that she had another mask on the other side of her head and another whole costume. I had only one mask; my varying thoughts had no influence on it. "I hate Ben. I love Ben," I said to the mirror. No change. Ticker-tape headlines, unframed fragments, loose from me. I made faces— sad, funny, happy. The mask was elastic. It resumed its original structure. It was a dead face. I tried to cry. Dry. It reminded me of trying to make myself vomit with the old finger-in-the-throat trick. I couldn't stand the idea. That reminded me of my mother insisting I have an enema, who knows what for; it was one of her favorite remedies. Lying on the bathroom rug prone while she pumped me with water and terrible pains and terrible fears that I wouldn't be able to hold it until she let me sit on the toilet. I got the same inner jitters now that I'd always had during the enemas, and they clashed so with my external, rigid, calm that I took one of the Libriums Ben had left in my medicine cabinet and deserted the mirror. Had this ever happened to anyone else, this detachment of the inside from the outside, this abominable condition in which the jitters razz at your heart like tiny elfin hecklers and nothing shows through on your skin, in your eyes? Your nostrils don't flare, your teeth don't grit, your hands don't shake even though they feel as if they want to. What do people do when they feel like this? Do they keep on living, supported by sheer habit? Do they take Librium and go to bed?

I decided I should lie still and perhaps the hecklers would go to sleep. Lying still, I discovered the need for movement. I massaged my mask, working the skin on my face in swirls, working it into expressions, until finally the glue began to loosen and the tears came and the numbness began to wash away.

In my sleep a balloon, a large wonderful balloon which defies the laws of gravity. I lie on it, draped in a comfortable curve. Me and my balloon alone in the sky, traveling slow motion in an arc, tracing a rainbow. We swing down toward earth, almost to the ground, but out of reach. Then begin an ascent, moving away with the caress of the breeze. I feel my body dressed, coated in the silk of soft hair. Below, a figure running on the ground. A tall man, not related to me, shouting, "Get off that thing. You can't do this to me." I slide my legs down, showing how impossible that is because as I do my arms pull forward and my balloon turns under me. I am still on top. I belong here. Getting off is prevented by some law of physics which I never appreciated before. I belong, here, to the air, where I can feel myself.

I woke light, the burden of my head relieved, the fresh air of blue skies lingering in my lungs. I drifted to the swing of my beginnings, the first recollection of my life—the swing in the side yard hanging from the maple tree my father said was one hundred years old. Low enough to the ground for me to get on alone. I was three years old and I clenched the ropes with my chubby fists and I felt the red curls on my head swing to the pull of gravity. I felt comforted by the back and forth motion. I felt the tenderness of the breeze, my weight on the branch, the melodious crunch of the ropes.

EIGHT

One part of me sat still and tracked the rest of me as I wandered around my apartment. It seemed barren; I had taken too much of my stuff to Ben's. And I was used to having someone watch me live. I decided it would be best to get the details out of the way, no loitering over the love I couldn't even recall for sure that we'd ever had. I called in sick at work, then waited until after nine to call Ben's and make sure he wasn't home.

No answer. Predictable that Ben should have splashed around in his grief with me until the wee hours of the morning to be sure to be done with it in plenty of time for his day at the office. Pleading with that 2 A.M. exhaustive statement— "I don't know if I'll be able to live without you, Francie." It was not the first time he'd dropped that threat for my consideration.

I sat with my second cup of coffee, looking through my window gate, across the dumpy backyards at the window gates of the others, the residents of Perry Street. There were curtains drawn across the windows of the third floor apartment directly across from mine, the one that had always been curtainless before. I must have lost my old neighbor. New York's privacy could be chilling sometimes, biting at you like the winter wind whipping off the Hudson and blustering down the narrow streets.

Jesus, God, what if I went there and found Ben dead? Laid out flat the way he always slept in the coffin position, limp and beginning to smell. Next to him strewn on my side of the bed, empty plastic pill containers. Pills—that would be the only possibility—he never liked anything messy. I imagined him fumbling with the containers, finally dumping all the pills on the bed. Fumbling because of his anger, which is not to say he was well coordinated under normal circumstances. He'd be saying to himself, "People aren't worth shit. That's you too, Francie. I thought you were more but you're the worst of all. I'll make you feel bad, because if anyone ever knew how much I needed them, it was you."

I picture myself standing alone at his funeral, so heavily weighted with gloom that it is best to stand still where I am though the others all stand together across the casket from me. Gravity hugging me so tight that I can't walk, I feel as if I must be wearing fishing boots, filled with water. I am terribly sorry for Ben at the same time that I hate him. A piece of me is being buried. I rage silently at his dead, yellow face, the bones more protuberant than I had ever imagined possible. "You should have warned me. I would've at least declared outright that I'd take no responsibility." I cry for myself. I didn't do it. A part of me is cold and observant and notices once again the leanness of his body and registers the fact that it would make a fine cadaver in an anatomy lab—the skinny ones are the best. If I could peel open his lids the look in his eyes would say, "This is the pay-back."

When I was seven a little girl in Otis died of leukemia. Linda Gladstone, daughter of the school principal, only five, her skin, baby-soft and her hair, white-blonde. I got up on my toes to stare into her casket and she looked peaceful and beautifully delicate, but she was dead. I was only convinced of her deadness because she was lying so stiff and flat on her back and I didn't think anyone ever slept that way.

The whole town was out for the funeral. My mother was crying and my father, who looked very strange wearing a suit, was holding his hands behind his back and rocking back and forth on his feet as if he were standing on hot pavement. I heard one of the teachers say, "It was a blessing in disguise," and I remember figuring that meant Linda was going to have a pleasant sleep for what should have been the rest of her life. So I didn't feel sad for her but I was very sorry for myself that it wasn't me. Then I started thinking about ways to kill myself, falling off a cliff in the cavern or getting run over by a car, but nothing seemed as good as leukemia which left you all in one piece and lying there peaceful and pretty for everyone to mourn over. If she hadn't already died, I think I would have taken to hanging around her to try to catch her leukemia.

I imagined my parents beside themselves for days, Mother wringing her hands and saying, "Poor Francie, she was so sweet and her life was just beginning." Dad, not being able to talk about it, would nod agreement and go on with the chores, and Megan would lie in bed at night and ask forgiveness for all the times she'd been mean to me. Only Joey, I imagined, would understand that I was better off and maybe even wish it had been him.

I unlocked the door to Ben's apartment. It was quiet except for the roar of the bus taking off outside. I checked the bedroom—no body. No horror. I let out all the air I'd been saving up in my lungs and felt the light-headed relief of escape.

I opened all the drawers and started popping my belongings into shopping bags. When I got to the records and other things we had bought together, I made decisions as if I were sorting poker chips. One for me, one for you. No special attachments allowed. I was seeing these things exactly for what they were—possessions. You go in the bag, you stay on the shelf. I felt exhilarated by my clarity. Only by noticing its absence did I realize that I'd expected the fog again, the fog as it had rolled in after Dad had been lowered in the hole.

The clunk of finality and then the haze fuzzing the senses.

The only time I felt like a voyeur was when I opened his underwear drawer to make sure none of my things were in there.

I stood by the curb with my paraphernalia and scanned the street for a cab. I had the distinct feeling of being unrooted, light, as I had been on my balloon in the dream. I waved down a checker cab. The driver breathed impatiently as I slid my suitcase and five shopping bags, one by one, across the back seat, but I took my time, aware of the monumental nature of my move. His rasping breath sounds penetrated the bulletproof shield. There was always the possibility that he had emphysema and breathed that way all the time.

Olee, Olee in Free. I was home safe again. Exhausted by the stairs and the bags, but still the energy in my limbs wanting for a target, jittering to be let loose. I could've called someone, but no, I felt as if I hadn't been alone in years. To share this experience would be to dilute it. If there were warring factions in me, then let them come out and keep each other company.

I had an inspiration. I'd paint my damned, dingy little kitchen. Two coats. It would take up the rest of that day and all of the next. Whatever mourning I had to do would end when the job was finished. The way it worked out, the mourning was over before I even got started, because when I went to look for my paint pants I discovered they were missing, and after conducting a thorough search, I had no alternative but to entertain the idea that Ben had probably thrown them out. He had always despised them. It was the lowest of the lowly things he might have done, but I was instinctively sure that he had done it. I painted with fury; the image of his long body, his hair tucked behind his ears, his soft lips, anything I might have conjured up to suit my need for nostalgia, vanished, and I saw only his bony hand strewing the trash over my soft, wadable dungarees, evenly distributing the balled up, used tissues to cover every inch of the faded blue, paint speckled, indestructable denim. In my rage I was spreading the paint on thick, each stroke covering three inches of grease spots. When had he done it? Any time in the past three months, since the last time I helped him paint something. He'd managed to intimidate me into not wearing those pants unless it was a painting occasion. Had he done it after I had walked out? As a last gesture of possession?

Anger inflamed my pores. Words gurgled in my guts and I let them out, cursing loudly so I could hear myself over the sound of the music on the radio. What kind of a fucking bastard would throw away someone's favorite pair of pants? He didn't think I was someone. Now he knows. He never knew me. He never let me be. My hostility valve open, hissing like a steam radiator at the whole male world, I felt life coming back into me, prickling at the listless limbs I'd draped around Ben. It was so different, painting with the High Gloss White and letting in the certainty that I would be able to see my reflection in it when it dried, from the way it had been after Dad was gone.

I wanted all of it, every ounce of animation that was coming to me, but I had to keep it from coming too fast by holding the rhythm of my paint brush to a metronome steadiness. On the second day, it was like doing the last part of a jigsaw puzzle, when suddenly everything begins to fit and you want to speed up your pace and rush to the end, only you try to hold back because you don't want it to be over so quickly. Also, you have the nagging suspicion that there will be a piece or two missing.

The missing pieces between me and Mom left us standing on opposite sides of a fault, an echoless chasm. I wanted to scream across the miles to her, "You, with all your preaching about making the best of things, you never made the best of it. You could have played out the tragedy on your piano. He wasn't there to put the lid down, to frown on your shiny, white keys, to assign you the washing of the eggs so that the lye was always threatening to burn your agile hands. You lived without him as if he were still standing over you. There are some things I need to tell you. . . if only you'd give me your good ear."

I sizzled with the will to do all the things Ben never wanted me to do. To play tennis well and not worry about the ego of the loser; to wear my newly designated paint pants seven nights a week until they got velvet soft and split in the rear; to eat chocolate chip cookies for breakfast and scrambled eggs for dinner; to catalogue all my past lovers by height, weight, color, tone of voice and major deficiency to see what I could glean from the collective experience; to clutter my apartment with junk mail for a week and then throw it all out at once in a flair of efficiency; to let a spider live in my bathtub; to pinch the toothpaste in the middle; to stock up on Dove soap and never see another cake of Ivory; to stare into so-called space for as many hours as I wanted to and not be accused of doing so-called nothing.

I would've started watering the dying Dracaena twice a week, too, but that was one of the things I'd left at Ben's.

NINE

Mother wrote me, sandwiching her sympathy in between
the news of Mrs. Dingle's nervous breakdown following the
birth of her seventh child and her own exasperating battles
with the old wringer washing machine which had once again
flooded the kitchen. She said she was sorry for me that it
hadn't worked out with Ben.

Sitting with her letter in front of me, I remembered the
day I got ice-balled off the pond by the big, bully boys. Running home and appealing to her with my beet red face, the
heat of the kitchen steaming my outrage so that it poured out
in tears. "Put your things on the radiator to dry and go wash
your face with cold water," she had said.

"No," I said. "I'm going back out." I ran down to Zeke
and Debbie's and listened hungrily to Mrs. Lester barking out
her anger on the phone at the boys' mothers. "You tell that
sorry son-of-a-bitch of a son of yours to pick on someone his
own size next time or I'll give him some of his own medicine."
Mrs. Lester was substantially large. By now the birthmark
that covered half of Zeke's right cheek, which had turned
bright purple while we had been ducking the ice balls and
taking our skates off, had gradually come back to brown.

Was it too late to let Mother console me? Friday night I
caught the six o'clock bus. I plopped into a window seat,

tossed my book onto the aisle seat and assiduously avoided eye contact with the approaching passengers. People, especially large people, like to sit with a small person. That was me. But for once I won the battle of body language that goes into seat selection. Then I curled up in the seat and let the hum of the tires on the highway lull me into a reverie of soft, whispered dreams. I thought—of course, Mother will understand my leaving him. She'll love me for having the courage to do it.

It was futile to try to talk in the car, Mom driving with her good ear facing the window and me riding with my good ear against the passenger window. I had discovered in college that I had a hearing loss too, while trying to earn extra money as a guinea pig in psychology experiments. Though I only heard half the tones, I got all the shocks.

Mother pointed proudly to the new McDonald's near the bus station. Progress. I decided not to bother trying to explain what Nathan's had done to the Village. We crossed the bridge and rode in silence out the Old Otis Road. There was the Old Otis Road, the New Otis Road and the Lake Road, the only roads I'd ever known until I went away to college. We passed my piano teacher's house on the left, but I couldn't tell if the porch swing was still there. Squeak, squeak, while inside Megan faltered at her scales, then played her piece and got a gold star, then sweat appeared on my palms as I waited for the door to open.

I had lost track of the curves in the road. I kept thinking we were rounding the curve just above our house, but then I'd see we weren't. We hadn't even passed the cemetery yet. Mother was never comfortable with silence. I was never comfortable not knowing where a road was going. Fortunately, it was only an eleven mile trip.

The Lester's barn came into sight on the left, its stubborn sag no worse than ever. It was as if both ends had started to collapse at the same time and impacted in the middle, leaving it with a stability just as good as that of a new barn.

"You see the eyesore is still standing," Mom said.

"Yeah. I always kind of liked it."

"God, it's horrible. I don't suppose they'll ever tear the darn thing down."

"Mrs. Lester wasn't scared to ream out the riffraff's mothers," I wanted to say, but didn't.

Carter's house had a fresh coat of green paint on the shutters. That was just as predictable as Lester's saggy barn. Our house looked smaller than I had remembered it, just like the psychologists say it's supposed to as you advance in age. Damn, I wanted them to be wrong. It didn't seem fair, given the fact that the confusion I'd left with ten years before hadn't shrunken with the size of the house.

Grandma Gerty was waiting up for me. She was warm and round and hugged me as if she really knew me, though she didn't. She knew the little girl who had listened raptly to her tea-leaf readings. She wanted to know why my cousin who lived in New York City had gotten divorced. "It's disgraceful," she said, before I could get my mouth open, so I didn't bother to answer. "I'll be off to bed now," she said, pressing me once more to her giant bosom.

While Mom put up the water for tea, I sat at the kitchen table and thought of late night talks when she had come through, mostly in my high school days. The time I'd told my first boss at the new *A & W* rootbeer stand what I'd thought of his boys-work-the-inside, girls-work-the-outside policy and had come home fired. She had sat with me until the sun came up, listening to me rant and rave about injustice, and then she'd told me the story of how she had lost her first job during the Depression and had gone on pretending to go to work for several days after, afraid to tell her parents the bad news. She'd let me sleep the next day and written me a sick-note for school.

She brought the tea and sat down. "So is it still off?" she asked.

"What?"

"You and this fellow?"

"Yes. I have no intention of renewing it."

"I don't understand. He seemed like such a nice guy."

"He was, the day you met him. If he was like that all the time, I'd have nothing to complain about."

"You know, I've always had the feeling about you, Francie, that you're looking for too much. You can't be too fussy. Nobody's perfect."

There it was. She didn't even want to know what was wrong with Ben. I felt my face flushing with anger. She didn't have any feeling for me; her regrets were for the wedding that wasn't going to come off. Of course I ask for too much. Who am I to expect someone not only to live with me but to recognize who I am and love me that way? How did I get so uppity as to not be overjoyed with just having someone to cherish and to service? I wondered what I could say to her. The words that kept repeating themselves to me were not accessible for audible speech. "Why don't you love me? Why don't you care about me? For once, why don't you stop worrying about the neighbors and what they might be thinking about your having an unmarried daughter close to thirty and worry about me?"

I could feel the tears rising through my hurt body and then dribbling down my cheeks. I caught her eyes and I glued myself to them. I felt naked and cruel, staring at her and knowing she wanted to say, "Go wash your face with cold water, dear," and not letting her, holding her silent with my stare until the question came out of me, "Why didn't *you* ever leave him?"

She sat very still but her lips moved, she was biting them, and her eyes stayed stuck on mine. I had the sensation of being partly inside her and I could feel the alarm going off in her. Then she said, "I never even thought of it."

I was astounded. I had been through this conversation so many times in my mind, but that had never been one of the answers. Yet, from the way she had said it, with that quiet, honest voice that she rarely ever used, I knew it was true. Then she went on. "Your Father was a good man in many ways, dear. He always provided for us and he loved you kids very much."

I wanted to sit and think about what that meant, the idea that she had never even thought of leaving him, but there was no time, she would wander back into a garden of trivia. "Why, Mom? Why did you put up with him coming home drunk all the time? I hated him when he bossed us all around."

"What else could I do?" she said. "I had you three small kids. I didn't know about his drinking until our honeymoon. Our first night married, he got so drunk he passed out. I was so shocked I didn't know what to do." I listened with full attention. The tears had dried on my cheeks. As she told about the honeymoon she let out a perverse giggle from time to time, as if to convince me that the inane situation she'd found herself in could be pardoned on the basis of its hilarity. The outrage that I kept thinking she should be feeling thumped at my temples.

The memory of him standing just inside the door with his wide, King Kong stance, flashed through me. All of us sitting polite and pretending no ill effects while our guts lurched and swayed with his stagger. "But didn't you tell him that you wouldn't put up with it? You didn't have to throw him out, but didn't you even ask him to stop? Did you ever tell him what it was doing to you?"

"I thought on the honeymoon that he was just celebrating, that he'd calm down once we got home and settled. He was a stranger to me in many ways but I'd married him and I thought, 'Now you have to make the best of it, for better or for worse.' He wasn't the kind of man you could ask to change. He had his ways and he expected you to take him the way he was."

"But don't you see how that wasn't fair, Mom? Why should you be the one to do all the bending? What if you'd said, 'Look, this is the way I am. I just can't tolerate you coming home sopping drunk.'"

"I didn't realize it affected you so. He would've been very distressed if he knew it. He loved you. I know it was hard for him to let you kids know, but he did."

"Sure it was hard. You didn't let him. You taught us not to go to him for anything. Not to expect much. You were the one capable of understanding us. He was there to collect the eggs. And he was Humpty Dumpty himself. I got the idea that if you ever knocked him down he'd break into a million, tiny, eggshell pieces and we'd never put him back together again. And that's what happened finally. One fall and he was gone. There weren't any pieces, just lots of blood. I remember when I saw him lying there, being astonished that he had so much blood in him. I'd never imagined he had anything in him. Hollow, I thought. A shell."

Mother flinched as though my anger was stinging her. Her age showed in the deep furrows going up from between her eyebrows and I felt bad that she was going to be old soon. She seemed very small though she was the same size as me. I softened my voice. "I guess I've been wondering ever since what he was really like. I'm not blaming you even if it sounds like that. He was cruel. It must've been terrible for you. He was so threatening when he was drunk, staggering around sort of aimlessly. I always thought he was just looking for something to hit. I wanted to hide in a corner. And you had to try to baby him up to bed, to get him out of our sight without making him mad."

"I'm sorry," she said. "Sorry you're so upset by all this. Sorry your father isn't alive. It's all past though. It won't help to harp on the past. I tried to do my best with you kids and I tried to do the best with my marriage. I wish I had it to do all over; I wouldn't make the same horrible mistakes I've made." The tone of her voice said, if you want to put me through the wringer, I won't resist. I've no defense. *Mea culpa, mea culpa*, I am at fault.

I am at fault—that was her defense. I lay in bed, anger numbing the sorrow I wanted to feel for her. How can you feel alive when you brush up against someone who, amorphous, slides from your touch? And yet she still holds the power to hurt. And worries about the neighbors.

"I never even thought of leaving him." That statement kept running through me. "You kids, you kids." She could never just say, "You, Francie." She might have thought of doing it for "you kids," but she'd never do it for herself.

Only she had. She'd had her one night out of the wings. But how could we ever speak of it as long as she had me muzzled by her *mea culpas,* as long as she thought I was too fussy, as long as anger could still render us both rag doll limp?

There were two standing family jokes about Grandma Gerty. One was that before Pappy died and she moved in to live with Mom, whenever she had invited anyone over for dinner, she always served meat loaf as dry as dog food. The other was about the way she trapped people who came to the house and lured them over to her scrapbook, and then told them her life story, whether they expressed an interest or not, by leafing through the photos and yellowed newspaper clippings. She'd gotten the Fuller Brush man, the Electrolux man, the blind piano tuner and any friend I'd ever brought home. Behind her back, we called it "Grandma Gerty's Show and Tell," and it always enraged Mom (though she'd never admit it) when Gerty stole her guests right out from in front of her.

Odd, then, that Mother, who had a lifetime habit of weighing the absolute necessity of every penny spent and who would have still been darning my socks if I had still been living at home, had taken Gerty's scrapbook out and had it very nicely rebound with leather so lovely it looked like it should be sitting on the Carter's coffee table. That was the lure. Once I had admired it properly, Gerty opened it to the same faded clippings and Mom rolled her eyes up in her head and breathed her exasperation sigh. Then, dustcloth in hand, she left the room.

"Ah, look at this, the old country," Gerty said, She reached out her arm, the flesh hung from the underside of it, and pulled me in closer, her arm and her shawl around my shoulder.

"Tell me their names again," I said, realizing I'd been through this narrative so many times before and yet I still didn't know it. Mom had taught me not to really listen, to pretend to be listening by providing my body as an audience, as she so often did.

"Gwillim, Abe, Margaret, Blodwin. . . ." She named her eleven brothers and sisters, the two rows of them in the picture, then pointed out the four who were still alive, and the hills in the background where the boys had gone off to the mines.

"My Mother had this photograph taken especially in honor of my going off to London, you know. I was just sixteen. She was very proud. It was most extraordinary for a young woman who'd grown up in the village to leave home, but I'd been chosen for a scholarship by the Royal College of Music in London. Oh, I was frightened, my dear. Mind you, I'd never been further than Cardiff, but I packed my case and off I went, eager to see London and to study with the very best people in the world. I was honored to have this fine voice, to have the whole family bursting with pride over me—they all had music in their hearts. What a thrill, my dear, you can't imagine."

But for the first time in my life I did imagine her excitement, and the way she rolled her "r's" was creating a small crescendo in my heart. Why had we always made fun of her? I wanted to say, "Go on, Gram, I'm really listening," only it wasn't necessary. She had already turned the page to a full size photo of herself. She handled the book as a priest handles a chalice.

She was beautiful in that photograph, beautiful and powerful. Her head was thrown back and her hair fell to her shoulders and her eyes were alive with the song. Her full throat was exposed and if you'd ever seen her sing, you could imagine it moving, jiggling at her control. From there down she was plump. She had always refused to be concerned about her weight, saying it was good for a singer to have a bit extra. I couldn't remember her rationale exactly—either it bouyed up your diaphragm or insulated you from cold so your voice would never freeze up.

She went on page after page. "Here I am singing in German. I think I've sung in just about every tongue. Here I am at the *Cymanfu Ganu* in Swanee." The *Cymanfu Ganu* was a Welsh song fest.

"Say it again, Gram."

"Ga-man-va-gan-i." She tested my pronunciation. I remembered her teaching me to count to ten in Welsh many years before.

St. Paul's. It was one of her high points. "Do you suppose you'll ever get to London, my dear?"

"Sure, maybe even this summer. I've been thinking about going," I said.

"You must," she said, "and you must visit St. Paul's. To imagine that magnificent cathedral being built, what a feat. And there I stood, alone. I felt so small, so honored. The sound of the organ was a gift of God. When I did my solo, my voice filled the space. I felt inspired to reach into every corner. I don't know how I did it, but I found myself lost in the song."

"It must have been quite a time for you," I said.

"Yes, a glorious time. It was the time of my life. I was invited here and there almost every day."

"Were you married to Pappy then?"

"I met him about that time, yes. He'd come to London to make his way and he had a little shop, a sort of stamp collector's exchange. We married and it wasn't long before we'd booked our passage to America."

I remembered when I'd first learned of the pilgrims and thought that she and Pappy must have come over on the *Nina*, the *Pinta*, or the *Santa Maria*.

"Did you want to stay in London?" I asked.

"Dear me, I don't even remember. Eniryn had a brother who'd already gone over and was living in Kansas. I had the world in my hands, and yet we came over with almost nothing. We'd no idea what was in store for us. We didn't even know where Kansas was. I was heartened after the long voyage by the excitement of New York, but then we went on to Kansas and found, to our great astonishment, there was nothing there. What an unblessed place that seemed after the rolling hills of Wales and the dignity of London. I was sick with loneliness and for the first time since I'd left home, I missed my family dearly. Eniryn saw, finally, that there was nothing there for him either, unless he was willing to take to the land, so we made the long journey back east, and then I began my career over again in New York.

She came to the clippings of her Broadway debut. "Ah, Ethel Barrymore. What a fine woman she was and what an honor to perform on the same stage with her." I knew she considered this the pinnacle of her life. The play was *The Corn is Green.* In one picture she stood proudly in her Welsh costume, Sunday best. It was a long dress, rather plain to denote her class, but covered in front by a fancy apron. Her hair was done up in a bun and topped with a high, black hat. In another she sat in the classroom leading the children in song.

"The theater was wonderful in those days. We worked hard indeed, but what a grand time we had. I don't understand what's happened to the stage. It's gone down so. Your mother reads me the accounts of people exposing themselves on the stage, as part of the production. My God, what's wrong with these people?"

"The plays are about a different generation," I said, but she wasn't paying attention. She'd gone on to the page of her doing the movie with Bette Davis and she was silent, looking far into the distance. Her body rocked ever so slightly, and as the frames of her life passed through her memory, a smile occasionally readjusted the lines of her face. Her wrinkles were monumental, but padded with the soft fat that insulated her whole body. Her face had a fluid look when it flowed with her reverie, as if no part of it was adherent. Finally she came back to me. "Well, dear, that's that."

"How come you never made any more movies after that?" I asked, knowing that I'd heard the answer before, but had lost the memory.

"Mind you, I could have," she said. "I was asked to, but I'd had three children along the way. William was the oldest, sixteen when I went out to Hollywood. I had a woman come in to look after them. When I got home, Eniryn had decided he didn't want me making any more movies. Pappy and I lived together over fifty years and that was the only time he really put his foot down. I suppose he was right. It wasn't fair to leave them all with some strange woman doing their cooking and cleaning up after them. I went on with my singing, mostly in the Episcopal church. He never tried to stop that. I'd had opportunities people don't have in a lifetime, and all by the time I was forty. Yes, I have to count my blessings. God knows what I would've gone on to if I hadn't stopped then."

There were a few empty pages at the end of the book. She brought the back cover gently down on them, then closed her eyes and ran her fingers over the soft leather of the binding, as if she were blind and feeling her life there. A lump welled up in my throat.

I watched Mother peeling the potatoes and pretended to have my ears open to her update on the neighbors. I detested my resemblance to her. Her wrinkles that were starting to form around my eyes, the way that my mouth looked when I forced a smile, the times I overheard my own voice and discovered I was quoting one of her lines. She had killed the whole day by running one chore into the next, while I had followed her around, watching, trying to sift out the contents of her life from mine. Sitting in that kitchen where familiarity and the towel stuffed along the back door sill both kept out the draft, I had a vision of Mother's icon—a woman with streaks of grey hair, frazzled at the ends, standing in union with a mop which she holds close, mop strings mixing with her hair and the dirty water from the kitchen floor running down her arm.

I wanted to say, "Mom, I almost killed him. Listen to me. If I had had the right weapon at the right time. . . ." But I said nothing. I remembered the feeling of the solid impact the morning Ben had blamed me for his over-sleeping—after I had gotten up and shaken him awake and reminded him he had an appointment with a client. I had gone up behind him in the bathroom while he had both hands occupied knotting his tie, and I had hit him as hard as I could with my fist in the middle of his back, shrieking at the same time, "Leave me alone. It's not my fault." It had been an alien voice, so shrill that I felt as if every cell in my body had been shattered by it. He had stared at me as if he hadn't understood I'd been in the house all along.

Mom got my attention by changing her voice to a whisper. "Did you notice how senile your grandmother's becoming?"

"No," I said. "I don't think she's senile. She's caught in the past."

"You don't have to live with it," she said. "She doesn't remember from one minute to the next. I have to treat her practically like a baby. God, it irks me the way she goes through that scrapbook over and over again."

"She should have gone on making movies," I said.

"I'd like to burn it and see what she'd do then."

Mother made a feeble attempt to mask her bitterness with a thin smile, but I could feel its acidity eating at the walls of my stomach. "Choose sides, choose sides." I could hear that cry echoing in my ears from the softball field, bouncing off the shellacked gymnasium floor, mixing with the sound of brisk cards being shuffled.

I refused to take sides. "I think I'll go for a walk before dinner," I said.

It was snowing. The grey clouds were chasing the sun off the horizon, but the sun held a strip of westerly sky and turned it lavender. It seemed suddenly all so clear how this chain had put a yoke on all of us. Mother struggling so futilely to be what she thought Gerty wanted her to be—obedient, dutiful wife and mother. She had tried, one had to credit her for that, and how could she be expected to know that duty wasn't what Gerty wanted anyway, even if she thought it was the only way to be. Gerty knew what it was like to sing her soul into the corners of St. Paul's Cathedral. Never mind that she had inverted that sweet glory into bitter duty; much as she needed someone to follow her ways, she could never heartily approve them.

I stood with my face turned up to the clouds and let

the snowflakes land on me, gentle caresses. Little wonder, I thought, that Mom should need me to imitate her life, omitting her one night out of the wings, of course. Wasn't there something in each of us calling out to someone, "Do as I do. Stamp me approved. Follow me and prove that I was valid." I could do it, find a man, cast myself as his wife and get on with my part. I knew the right lines, had the smile down pat. Mom would be pleased. But would she? And for how long after the glorious telling of the neighbors?

Regardless, I wouldn't. The yoke was off. I would not run on the end of the whip. I would refuse the game. Her icons would have to drown in their own mop water.

TEN

At the bus station Mother and I stood a couple of feet apart, facing each other but glancing about for familiar faces. The awkwardness of each of us waiting for the other to reach forward to initiate a parting embrace, to reinforce our tie even though it remained twisted, was an awkwardness we knew well. It was a sensation we had lived with ever since Dad's death, but one that did not lose its edge with time and regularity.

I was not going to do what she wanted me to do with my life. That meant I owed her the first move. The daughter who breaks the chain becomes the mother. I stepped into the chasm, opened my arms and enclosed her. She patted my back as if I were still the daughter. "I love you," she said.

"Take care of yourself," I said. I could not say more. Of course I had taken for granted that I loved her as a child. But what did it mean, now, to say I loved her when I knew so little of her? And what I did know provoked so many feelings that I couldn't sort them out. I grabbed my suitcase and ducked through the bus door, found a seat, then watched her searching for my face behind the smoke-grey windows. She found me and waved. We were so much more comfortable this way with the thick pane shadowing us. The bus driver revved the engine. Mother threw a kiss. I was left with my desire for a full embrace.

If Mother had known I was a witness, would she still have bought the accident theory? I would never know. I suspect the neighbors would have pushed it on her whether she wanted it or not. They all wanted it, even Ethel, whom I loved. No one could wait to clean up the blood. In fact, that was one of the many things I had never found out—who actually did clean up the blood? I didn't know who had arranged to have the chickens carried off either. Or who had the chicken shit shoveled out of the barns. Or who got Mom a job at the feed store. Otis was a small town. People took care of you. Maybe Ethel. Ethel didn't know anything about chickens. Maybe Charlie. Charlie knew about insurance and Dad had always had insurance. He kept it in a strongbox which he took out about twice a year. Dad would spread the papers all over the kitchen table and not let anyone near them. Could you collect life insurance if you were convicted of manslaughter? I didn't have any idea.

Without ever stating it, Mother had set a policy of not talking about any of this. After the funeral she took to chatting a lot about nothing, or at least nothing that mattered to us. So and so came into the feed store today and guess what he told me?

"What?"

"You know that barn that burned down on the Wallace place out on the old Otis Road? They think it was set."

"Muriel Beatty's mother broke her hip. She's gone in the nursing home. Once they go in like that, it's a wonder if they ever get back out."

She came home from work every night at five-fifteen. We came home from school at three-thirty, and she'd call up around quarter-to-four and ask us what homework we had and suggest we go ahead and do it. Sometimes she'd ask Megan or me to put something on for dinner. We learned to cook by telephone.

"Get out the big, black frying pan. Cover the bottom with Crisco. Melt it. Put it on medium heat. Then. . . ."

"How can I possibly remember all this, Mom?"

"Okay. Go get the pan. Do the Crisco. I'll hold on."

I would return to the phone. "What do you mean by medium heat?"

"The fat shouldn't snap and crackle. You just want it hot, but not sizzling. Now you want to dust the pot roast with flour, a little salt and pepper. I've got to go take care of someone. Go dust it. I'll call back."

Often the line was busy when I was ready for the next step. We had six parties on it and at some point they each contributed to our cooking education.

When Mother got home she would make the gravy and put dinner out on the table which was already set. She sat at the end where Dad had sat before. But no matter where she sat, she was no longer the heart of our family. No one was. She told us the details of the lives of people who came through the store. She brought home the cloth, print feed bags that had been returned, empty, and made our clothes out of them. She scared us with her unspoken fragility, which really belonged to us all. You couldn't embrace her fully because she never seemed whole.

Pappy retired and he and Grandma Gerty moved to our village the year after Dad died. "Because the country was so beautiful," they said. They kept a close eye on us. They came to our house and joined in the conversation of the endless details. I was hoping they would be the ones to push for more, but of course they couldn't. No one wanted to intrude. Grandma Gerty sang while she dried the dishes. My spine chilled. Her voice was loud and joyful. It pierced our silence and I feared it might break the glasses.

They had only been living in Otis a few months when Pappy had his stroke, a disastrous one which left him without speech, without apparent comprehension, and with severe paralysis of his right side.

They lived three houses down from the school and in the direction Debbie and I had to walk to get home. There was nothing I could do to help, but Mother said, "Stop in. Just stop as you pass the house and say hello. Have a cup of tea with your grandmother. She likes to see your face." That meant I should smile while I was at it.

"But I have to study Biology with Debbie," I would say.

"You don't have to stay long."

But I didn't know how to leave once I got there. Pappy couldn't talk, yet I had to say goodbye to him. If I went over and took his hand, he would nod, his face would collapse and he would cry. Grandma Gerty didn't sing in his presence. Debbie came with me once, but as soon as she finished her cookie she rolled her eyes toward the door. She didn't understand that I was stuck with these people, that I was helpless to turn my back on them, to run off gleefully with her. I felt betrayed the next day when we got to their door and she said, "See you later. I'm not going in there. Your grandfather looks like a ghost." But betrayed or not, I agreed with her and only went myself because I had to.

I had done this visiting for a couple of weeks before Mr. Springer started coming on Tuesdays and Thursdays. He was the first physical therapist I ever met. He had seven children, and half of his stomach had been removed because of ulcers. He could only eat mush, but Grandma Gerty couldn't seem to remember that and kept offering him tea and cookies. The most amazing thing about him was that he knew what to do with Pappy. With his strong arms and his half a stomach, he would swoop Pappy up out of his chair and shuffle him down the hall to the bedroom, making him carry his own urinal slung over his spastic arm. Then he would talk him through his exercises without asking for any answers. He kept up a steady stream of conversation and it didn't seem to bother him at all that it only went one way. He laughed at whatever it was they were doing together. Sometimes Pappy laughed in return, sometimes he cried. Mr. Springer was the only one around who didn't seem helpless; he walked as if he had springs in his toes.

On holidays we all trooped down to their house because Pappy couldn't get up our stairs. We'd prepare the meal at home, then carry it on our laps in the car. Grandma Gerty and Mom would prop Pappy with pillows in the captain's chair at the head of the table. This was a change of pace from the wheelchair, in honor of the holiday. Mother sat at the other end of the table. Grandma Gerty sat next to Pappy on one side and I got stuck next to him on the other, because Megan and Joey beat me to the table. Grandma Gerty cut his meat into tiny bits and covered it with lots of gravy since he had trouble chewing. I wondered why they didn't just feed him Mr. Springer's mush. Once Grandma Gerty was finished fixing his plate, she didn't pay much attention to him. Out of the corner of my eye I watched him drool the gravy and lost my appetite.

Mother kept her full attention on him all the time. She sat with the pies and the spatula in front of her.

"Now Dad, you don't have to answer. Just nod your head. Do you want apple or pumpkin?"

A groan of despair came out of him.

"Mom, you can't ask that way," I said.

"Okay, okay. Dad, just yes or no. Do you want pumpkin?"

"No, no, no, no, no. . ."

She interrupted him before he got the no to stop. "Apple? You want apple then?"

"No, no, no, no, no."

"No pie. You don't want pie?"

"No, no, no, no, no, no."

"Does that mean yes, you want pie?"

Tears in his eyes.

"Mom, cut him a piece of pumpkin. I'll try it," I said. I put it in front of him. He ate it. When we were leaving and I went to shake his good hand and kiss his good cheek, he said, "Yes, yes, yes, yes, yes." Did he remember that I had gotten him a piece of pie? I thought he might, but I was not sure the way that Mr. Springer was, when he asked questions that didn't need the answers.

When I was fifteen I wrote in my English composition that I was going to be a physical therapist, then I forgot, so that when I got to college I didn't think I knew what to be. I went through the catalogue and by process of elimination, I thought, I ended up majoring in physical therapy.

ELEVEN

"Good morning, Mr. Simpson."

"Yes, dear. Good morning."

"Ready to go? Think you can make it out to the hall today?"

"Oh no, no, dear. Don't get too ambitious. Never pays."

"Be right back. You get ready. Lock your wheelchair."

"It's quite all right, dear. Take your time. No rush for me. Maybe we could just skip today."

Did he mean skip walking or skip the whole day, I wondered? Ostensibly ignoring the comment, I moved with the efficiency of one who has an important, last minute task to do and ducked into the office to finish my coffee. The thing about Simpson was that he was sapping me. He had suffered his stroke while fucking a strange woman. My sympathy went to her and to his wife, but my energy went to him and he was a sieve. He was absorbing all my resources without being touched by them. Basically, he seemed to want to be left alone to rot, but that would have meant my own admission of defeat and I preferred the discomfort of experiencing my sadistic impulses. The only thing that seemed left unbent in him after his stroke was his politeness. Tall manners that crippled my sadism, that permeated the air around him as he sat, eyelids drooping, determined that his present condition was permanent destruction, reiterating the perfection of his pre-morbid world. As far as I could see he'd always been a loser.

I bent over him, preparing him to stand. His black hair hung in globs, third stage, unwashed, hospital hair. The first stage is grease, its thick molecules holding small strands, peppered with dandruff. Then the rank odor, haloing a two foot circumference of the head. Finally, the strands bond into globs.

"Mr. Simpson, why don't you ask the nurses to wash your hair? It can be done, you know."

"Yes, yes I will." He looked away, irritated. I was intruding upon his private life again. He didn't think it worth the trouble.

"Okay, up," I commanded, lifting him at the same time and jamming my knee into his on the paralyzed side to make him straighten up. Balancing in this position, pushing hard to pass the sadistic impulse from my leg to his, aligning his bones, segment over segment to pass his weight back to him, without his noticing, was the task at hand. For as soon as he would notice, his whole body would droop, thinking it calamitous that his legs should be capable of holding him up. It was our daily routine, his noticing, drooping, my desire to goose him preoccupying at least one whole convolution of my brain. Coaching him and balancing him, I got the cane into his hand and eeked the steps out of him—tiny, tedious efforts to move forward. Constantly realigning the droop. "Come on, Mr. Simpson, you can do better than that. You're leaning on me."

"Enough, we've done enough. Let's sit down."

"No, you've just started. You're leaning on me again. Stay up."

He was folding, unnecessarily, out of total lack of interest. My voice rose to a pitch that startled us both. "Mr. Simpson. Straighten yourself out. You're heavy. I'm getting stronger and you're getting weaker, that's all we're accomplishing." I sounded like an angry commandant of deaf troops.

His obedience silenced me. He stood shockingly tall and

straight and walked amazingly well for his condition. Out of fear or etiquette, I didn't care. Awed by his new air of dignity, I remained silent, and escorted him out to the hall and back. Seated, he breathed relief.

"Wow, that was great," I said.

"Not bad, eh?"

"Not bad at all. I knew you could do it."

He fumbled for his handkerchief and wiped the tears from the corners of his eyes. Looking up, his eyes fully open for the first time in my presence, fluid brown, he said, "Do you think I'll get better?"

"Much better. I'm sure you'll get much better," I said with conviction.

I saw Kristin being wheeled down the hall. I waved at her even though I still faced Simpson. I was glad she was next on my schedule on this particular day when Simpson had finally decided to give something back.

Kristin came twice a week and exercised in the Hubbard Tank. I had worked with her for three years, although according to her prognosis, she was not supposed to have been living past the first. Her birthdays took on weighty significance and this was her fifteenth. I transferred her over to the stretcher, then rolled her from one side to the other and removed her robe. She came in her own bikini because she hated the grey, cloth suit that the hospital supplied. I lifted her head gently and placed the rubber pillow under it just above the lump that protruded from the base of her skull. I removed the scarf she wore to cover her baldness so that it wouldn't get wet. She had some thin, blonde hairs on her scalp, new growth. I had an impulse to kiss the top of her head, but of course, I didn't. I pushed the button on the hoist that elevated the stretcher and swung her out over the water.

"Ready?" I asked.

"Guess so," she said.

I lowered her into the tank of warm water that would relax her muscles and make her movements easier. I walked around the tank adjusting the jets of water on her legs. "How are you feeling?" I asked.

"It's my birthday."

"Yeah. I know. Happy Birthday."

"I'm getting oh-wuld." She had some problems with her speech which made the "old" sound like a two syllable word.

"Old and decrepit," I said because I had taken her arm to help her move it, but she held it down. "Come on, let's do these exercises."

"Let's not," she said. "Since it's my birthday, don't you think we should just lie here and pretend we're at the beach?"

"You're in the water. I'm out here."

"Tough luck," she said.

This was part of a regular battle-game that Kristin and I played together.

"Come on. Let's get started," I said, more seriously.

"What if I don't want to?"

"You have to."

"No, I don't. What if I won't?"

"I'll get mad."

"So what."

"So what. . . okay, you think you've got me. If you don't. . . ."

"What? How are you going to make me?"

"I'll turn the cold water on in the tank." It was a threat I had never thought of before. I walked to the faucets at the far end. Just as I got there she kicked vigorously with her uncoordinated legs and splashed me quite thoroughly. We both laughed while I dried myself. Then she did her exercises.

She was staying for lunch which was actually her birthday party. I left her with the aide to get dried off and dressed and went to change my white coat. The aide came to get me. "Kristin says to tell you that you forgot something," she said.

I went back to the hydrotherapy room. "It's not like you to ask for extra treatment," I said. "You must be sick."

"You forgot to measure me," she said.

"Actually I didn't forget. I thought you should take a week off. It's your birthday."

"Come on. Get your tape," she said.

I marked on each side with a skin pencil, the place where the brain tumor started to protrude. Then I drew the yellow tape across its most prominent part and took the measurement. I gave the figure. My fingers wanted to stretch the tape but I didn't let them because Kristin said, as she did each week, "Are you sure?"

"I'm sure," I said.

Kristin had the guts I needed when I went home each night after work. I was trying to establish routines that would guarantee my going on alone. I had passed from a state of exuberance over not having to be home at a certain time for Ben to a state of anxiety over having only myself to confront when I got there. Usually I was tired; I treated twelve to fifteen people in a day. I needed ways to share the feelings I came home with. One way I found was to write a journal, to sit with a notebook and a haze in my head and awkwardly, self-consciously search for words that would explain my life to me.

The other way was to find company and mostly I found Lisa because our lives were so parallel. I went to her place, she came to mine, or we walked or ate out or went to movies. We went to the C.R. group once a week. The other women there seemed pleased that I was finished with Ben, but didn't have many answers to my problems with living alone.

I had my cozy apartment with my freshly painted kitchen and I had my enlightened vision of my ancestral cage. My apartment was hardly adequate, but it was rent-controlled and the rent had frozen at one-hundred-and-fifteen a month. I took a thorough survey of its possibilities. The kitchenette was a corner of the living area with stove, oven, and sink crammed into a space less than three feet wide. A normal size dinner plate would not lie flat in the sink, which was only about six inches wide. A turkey would not fit into the oven. I had bought one once and had to cut off the legs and cook them separately. My apartment had high ceilings with exposed beams, and a fireplace. That always seemed impressive until

I told people about the super who lived upstairs and who threatened to brick the fireplace over if ever I burned wood in it again. It made his place smell like smoke, he said.

I had an alcove for my bed and one long closet with a small door which was partially blocked by the bed. I had some makeshift furniture, most of which had been given to me when I'd first moved in. I decided to look at this place as the place I was going to live in forever, like the old woman who lived below me. When I carried her groceries up for her one day, she told me to call her "Mama."

"Do you have children?" I asked her.

"No. Cats." She took in strays. The odor in her apartment made me hold my breath. She had lived there for forty-five years. One of her cats followed me up the stairs. I took it back down to her, but she didn't close her door. Another came out and followed me. I had to push it away with my foot to get in and close the door. I was going to learn how to live there forever. Mama was my model. I went out and bought a couch. I shopped and cooked and tried to figure out ways to make eating alone not feel sad.

I cared a lot about my work and sometimes I walked as if I had springs in my feet. I knew how to talk to someone who couldn't talk back, but my grandfather had died before I had finished college. I didn't know how Mr. Springer felt, but when I had to do something like measure Kristin's tumor, I still felt at a loss.

TWELVE

The city winter dragged on and seemed by its nature to push people into further isolation. In spite of the stiff, dry shrinkage of my sinuses from the steam heat indoors, there was the question—Is it worth it to go out? Would I feel victimized by the wind whipping my face and the cold numbing my fingers?

I called Lisa. "Come on over," she said. "See if you can find any scrap wood on the way."

She had a fireplace which she could use. Once I was out and walking down the street, I was so pleased with myself for getting out, I forgot to look for the wood.

Lisa was in one of those moods in which she made a great deal out of her sense of loss of Arthur. Sometimes when she did that, I thought perhaps I had buried that sense in me and tried hard to let it surface, but nothing came, only the feeling that Ben's absence provided breathing room—vital, exhilarating space to stretch and take full breaths in. Lisa had, after all, deserted Arthur for herself, and she would come back to that finally, even in these moods.

"I've never really been on my own before," she kept saying. "I'm learning a good deal about myself."

"I'm learning too," I said, "only I'm tired of learning. I want to wake up elated some morning."

"I've got Arthur's car this weekend. Want to get out of the city?"

"Of course. I'd love to. Where would we go?"

"Skiing. Vermont."

We drove to Vermont, the skis clamped down tight in the rack above us, the wheels slipping sideways as we crept up the hill to the parking lot of the mountain.

Riding the chair lift to the top, I was excited but miserable. My toes crushed in the rigid boots, the clumsy feeling of my hands covered with thick gloves causing me apprehension that I might drop my poles, my scarf not on just right, leaving a slit where the cold wind was blowing on the back of my neck just above my collar. "It's going to be great," Lisa said.

"It better be," I said. And then we were off the lift and standing ready and I felt the eagerness swell in me, the cold, fresh air slapping me awake, one thousand times awake, alert to all sensations and they were all delicious. The setting of my muscles the way I wanted them, the smell and the taste of freedom, the abandonment of fear. I pushed off with elation and as the mountain took me, I delighted both in controlling it and having it control me. I fell, laughing, embracing the soft, white ground, my slippery protector and demon. Pain was on another planet. "It's wonderful," I called to Lisa. "Do you love it?"

"Yes," she said. "Come on. More." My feelings were visible in her eyes and expressed in the exuberance of her voice. Charged, we went on all day, up and down. Feeling the fatigue on the way up, losing it to the wind at the top, savoring all—the valley below, sun rays caressing the stick figures of trees, speed that pitches the heart to a high note.

Oblivious to the other skiers, we hollered back and forth to each other. "Watch me." I stopped and watched Lisa. She bounced rhythmically, turning from side to side, her skis held together effortlessly. She was much better than I. She passed me, aware of the seductive grace of her body. "You are superb. Now, watch me," I called, "if you want to see a gazelle." I made a few good turns, the right, crunching sounds under my feet feeding my smile, and then I tumbled at Lisa's feet, my skis flipping over me, leaving me tangled. I was filled to a spilling point with love, able even to be enamored of my awkward faults. We laughed loudly together and heard the valley echo our pleasure. "Come on, gazelle. Let's go."

How could it be that I had forgotten how much I loved to ski? I remembered my first time. Going up the chair lift with my good friend who wanted me to like it and finding the novice trail closed because of poor conditions. My knees shaking and the idea passing through my mind that I must be slightly crazed to attempt this, but then the time for alternatives was past. I didn't know how to stop or turn except by falling and rearranging the direction of my skis before I got up. So that's what I'd done, zig—fall, zag—fall, making a gradual descent. Jerry followed me, laughing at my tactic, but not doing so well himself. When we arrived at a short but very steep drop-off, I'd said, accusingly, "Why'd you bring me here?"

"I didn't know they'd closed the trail. How're we going to get down?"

"You're asking me? You go first. Then wait for me down there," I said. "At least there's a plateau to stop on at the bottom."

"I don't think I can do it. Let's side-step it. Come on, I'll show you how." He started sliding down, sideways, a few inches at a time. Others were joining him, off to one side.

"Fuck that," I said. "We'll be here all day." I faced my skis downhill and held myself back with my poles. Then I let go. The speed came instantly and I felt I must be flying except for the bumps which jiggled up through my legs, and my head reeled, overflowing with pride that I was still on my feet, that the hill was mine. Then I was on the plateau but my speed didn't slow, so I fell and lay back for a while in the snow, drinking in the feel of it, wishing to remain unleashed like that forever. Jerry finally turned and did the last third of the hill facing forward.

"I don't believe you," he said. "You're crazy." He was as impressed as I.

"I'm hooked," I said. "Let's go up again."

Lisa and I drove back to the motel with that fine sense of exhaustion that arrives when your exertion has been so dominated by pleasure that it becomes an energy, revitalizing even as it expends. We took turns soaking in the bathtub. I mused, lying immersed except for the rings around my nipples where they floated above the water line. What more could I want than to share my happiness with Lisa, who wanted it and was glad for me to have it. If only this could be my life, this day. The deprivation I had endured to keep Ben stood out in contrast, and for once it seemed to me that I had no need for men. I surveyed my body and found myself attracted to it. The white, soft skin of my breasts, the two arches formed by my pelvic bones and the flat space sloping off from them, the well demarcated lines of the muscles in my arms, developed to their optimum capacity from years of doing exercises with my patients. The warmth of the water soothed me from outside in; the warmth of my own acceptance, taking in even that mysterious, alien being who had needed Ben, soothed me from inside out. My eyelids drooped. Nearing a state of stuporous relaxation, I mobilized myself to get up and dry off.

Lisa was lying face down on her bed. She turned her face to me. "We're going to be sore tomorrow but it's worth it," she said.

"I haven't felt so good in a really long time," I said.

"I know. It was a great day."

"I forgot how good it could be. God, Ben even managed to make skiing a chore. The first time I took him up in a chair lift, I thought he was going to kill me. I didn't know he was scared shitless of heights."

"You should have."

"Yeah, you're right. It wasn't out of character."

"Poor old Ben. He didn't fare well under almost any conditions," she said. We laughed.

"I miss Arthur. We had some great times skiing. He loved it once he learned how. He was so vain, it was hard for him in the beginning. He hated looking awkward, but he was a natural so he got over that fast." She drifted away from me and into her memory of Arthur, and I was sorry I had brought up the subject by talking about Ben when it seemed such a perfect day for living without past or future.

I lay down on my bed and we were silent for a while. One wall of our room was glass, overlooking a smooth, white hill, dotted by trees at the bottom. The sun had gone while I was in the bathtub and the only thing that remained visible was a small mound of the hill, lit by a spotlight on the roof of the motel. The snow had a gleam like the enamel of a tooth. I remembered when I was a child, the wonder of going out to a fresh snowfall in the morning and seeing the smooth perfection of how it had covered everything evenly. I would be dying to jump into it and make my two deep foot prints as I'd sink to my knees or higher, but I'd make myself wait for a few minutes, protecting it from being adulterated. Then, if Joey came whooping out, yelling, "Wow, look at the snow," I'd say, "Wait, just look a minute," but by then he'd have jumped off the porch into it. He had no sense of reverence.

Lisa moved, groaning with a sound that triggered an alarm in me. It was a groan of desire and of pleasure. I had been set for it, but my anticipation had only served to wind me up, tight as a spring. "I can't move," she said. "Would you rub my back a little?"

"Sure." The alarm was still with me, a startling sensation along my inner thighs, and I worried that it might communicate itself through my hands as I touched her back. She parted her long, silky, black hair, flipping half to each side. It covered her face so I could only see her mouth, her smile, as I sifted her finely textured skin and taut muscles through my hands. I stopped worrying then and concentrated on the feel of her, and the sight of her, and gradually I found I wasn't so much massaging her as just stroking her skin and feeling my need for tenderness that must be in her too, and feeling I wanted to give and give and give to her all that was in my hands, until she wouldn't hurt from Arthur or anybody at all.

After a while I began to feel my own fatigue so I stopped, saying, "Okay, my turn. Would you do me?"

"Of course. That was super. Your hands are great."

I took off my robe and went to my own bed. She touched me gently. I was startled but held myself still, allowing the strong urge to recoil to stay within me, coiling me with excitement. Her hands were steady, never losing contact, and I eased into their rhythm, smiling and savoring the prickly warmth of arousal. There was a voice inside me struggling to get in a word, trying to tell me with some semblance of horror, "My God, you're acting like a lesbian." But horror was not allowed, was stroked off my back with a gentle brush as a feather duster dispenses a layer of settled particles. I wanted to turn over, holding out my arms to her, offering to draw her in closer to my tripping pulse, but no, the voice got in. She might be horrified. How do I know she feels the same way? And what will happen to us, to this fine friendship? I agonized, wishing for her to stop and wishing for her to go on. It seemed as though she was lingering, reluctant as I to sever this moment, this bond, which titillated me to desire more and at the same time was gratifying in and of itself. Then she ran her fingers through my hair, which was cut short, layered, so that as her hand passed them the hairs fell back down into place. There was care in her hand, and peace, so that I knew, by contrast, how many times I'd been touched by careless hands, by those who confuse passion with flinging, staccato bursts of movement.

She sat back. "Okay. How do you feel now?" she said.

"I feel just fine. That was wonderful." I turned over and let out an audible sigh as she moved away. Watching her walk about the room, taking her clothes out of the suitcase and dressing, I nodded agreement to her suggestions—dinner, check out the local movie. My body was putty except for the

quickening streak of desire that gripped at my heart. Her ski..
was tight, giving clear definition to the lines of her body.

She turned and caught me looking at her and neither of
us looked away. Then, with a faltering voice I'd never heard
her use before, she said, "Well, are you going to get dressed
or what?"

There must have been a million reasons, gathered over
the separate courses of our lives for letting this moment pass—
jokes and gossip, gestures and ill conceived remarks, grimaces
and gawking eyes. Years spent collecting heterosexual cre-
dentials. Friendship taboos tatooed on our brains, etched
deep with razor sharp care by all those who wished us to
join their straight-arrow club and keep things neat.

All these reasons were suddenly in the air, buzzing in
my head as if I'd bumped up against a bee's nest, and while
they couldn't take the tenderness out of her touch, they had
everything to do with the way we dropped our eyes and I
said, "Yes, I'm starving. I'll get dressed."

Our relief at having found a safe midstation was apparent as we resumed our friendship over dinner and let the
tension drown in fatigue from the full day. Still, I couldn't
help noticing that Lisa had the same mouth as Debbie, the
soft, full lips that had always given away how she felt, in the
days when Debbie and I hadn't used words but had known
there was harmony in our thoughts.

Debbie, with whom I had lain on an Indian blanket on
the unshaded side of the apple orchard and listened while
she read aloud the stories from *True Confessions* magazines.
I could remember nothing else from one whole adolescent
summer but us, taking off our blouses and feeling the warm
glow of sunshine on our new breasts, reading of how the
handsome, confident, black haired man took the girl, pierced
her for the first time, not hearing her cry over his heavy
breathing, and how, even as she hurt, the animal desire arose
in her. There was the gentle wind caressing my breasts and
the sweetness of Debbie's body, hairless and evenly tanned
except for her top, where my eyes always landed no matter

d to direct them, and the throbbing sensation, , between my legs, almost a pain. Always the sense , someone might come along and the darting glances, be. en paragraphs, in the direction of the dirt road. The stories were always the same except for details such as hair color, but that didn't keep us from reading the magazine through, cover to cover. Then we'd wonder out loud—How could these girls like something that hurt? The blondes, the brunettes, even the redheads, first felt the stabbing pains, then they liked it. With all our erectile tissues quivering, we vowed to each other that we'd hold fast to our virginity until we were quite sure that we were old enough to stand it—this brusque, coarse handling of our bodies.

Debbie didn't keep her vow. She told me she was pregnant the day we took our Senior Regents. It had been a sad mystery to me, visiting her each year while I was in college, the kids piling up and Debbie's voice rising to a new pitch to be heard above the din. After a while I couldn't stand to visit her anymore. I couldn't find the child who had followed my moods by feeling them as we had walked home from school together for twelve years. I couldn't find her at all.

Lost, gone under. But there she was resurfacing in Lisa, who sat across from me, her wide eyes teasing as she described my style of skiing, then the corners of her mouth soft with vulnerability as she talked of how easily she bruised.

THIRTEEN

The jet aimed at the sun, then leveled out, and I made a conscious effort to feel the distance the pilot was placing between us and the concrete island of Manhattan. I watched until it took on the perspective of the erector set project Joey and I had done after Mom had carted us off for our first view of New York City, Joey barfing all through the Catskills on the bus.

Then the white clouds were the floor beneath the plane and I stared, mesmerized. The snow of the sky. I dreamed about skiing, about Lisa's soft touch, her wish to come with me. She hadn't gotten the money together. But I had a sense of well being about the fact that I was going anyway, that I was treating myself to Europe because I'd survived a tough year and deserved a good vacation, that the two empty seats beside me were just that and not spaces for invisible hecklers to sit and jeer, "What are you doing alone?" It seemed ludicrous now to think back to a couple of months ago—to remember the first time I had gone to the movies alone. Standing in the block long line, pushing up close to the people ahead of me so I'd be likely to be identified as one of them, fingering my ticket so nervously in the long wait that I almost turned the paper back to pulp.

...n seemed stately and proud and the tenor of the ...rmeated the air I was breathing. At first I felt re-...oy it. Charming—strangers being courteous to strang-e... ...ne conductor on the red bus smiling and dispensing "Good Mornings" with his change, giving me directions to Hampstead Heath as if he were sending me out from the very center of civilization. No, he wasn't trying to seduce me; no, he wasn't going to lick his chops as I walked away; yes, that smile was habitually plastered on his face.

For the first few days I felt I was becoming domesticated. I was smiling back, holding my elbows tight down to my sides when passing others on a crowded bus, putting a whispy ring of morning sunshine into my voice. Then, all of a sudden one afternoon, I found myself tightly grasping the pole of the red bus to contain my desire to push someone off. It was Mother. She was this whole fucking society. It was her cerebral smile and her gentlewoman's agreement to guarantee no one step-ing on anyone else's toes. I wanted someone to scream be-cause it wouldn't be right for me to—I was only a tourist.

Way back in the ninth grade, I had visited a prison with my civics class. Perhaps it was the way the poles were ar-ranged on the back of the bus that reminded me of people in prison. But nothing had been painted bright red there—the building had been stark, raw concrete. We had gone through the men's section first. They were striped by their uniforms and by the bars, walking restlessly as monkeys in their cages, bent with lethargy but unable to wind down. I had thought of how much I had hated playing the lion in the circus play in third grade, being dragged across the stage in a cage. A few of the men called to us, some whistled sex calls, especially at Debbie. I had stayed between her and Helen, hiding myself from them and them from me, as much as I could.

Then we had gone to the women's area. They shrieked at us like loony birds—discordant cackles, obscene words, sounds of a barnyard of hysterical hens. They came to the window and squawked, trying to drive us away. Would they have put Mother in with these women? I needed to talk to them, to ask, "Why are you like this?" I kept Debbie and Helen behind, waiting until the rest of the class had moved on and the prisoners sounded as though they had roosted. Then I went back to the high, barred window, standing on my toes to see in. The blonde one, her wiry hair straggling in all directions from her head, her eyes enraged and tortured, stepped from the side of the window to scare me. Spitting her words directly into my face, she screamed, "Get out of here, you fucking snot. You've had your show." I felt stung, sorry I'd looked again, offending, accusing. I'd only meant to understand what was wrong with them. I turned away quickly and discovered that Helen and Debbie were gone. To me alone, that woman had been talking. I wanted to ask for a key so that I could be placed in the massive concrete cell and be one of the ones screaming out at the voyeurs, a belonger in that cacophonous orchestra. I wanted Mother to call out that way, telling off the neighbors, yelling "I did it. Yes I did. He drove me to it. Now just leave me alone."

I loosened my grip, dropped off the end of the bus and took another bus back in the other direction to move my flight reservation to Ireland up a few days. Then I went to St. Paul's Cathedral. I sat in the back, I sat in the middle, I sat in the front, and from each place I sat, I tried to picture Grandma Gerty. I understood why she had never worried about her weight. It seemed as if each additional pound made her singing here a more likely event by giving her a larger presence. Tourists' voices echoed off the walls. I closed my eyes and tried to hear Grandma Gerty's voice alone above the actual noises. I saw her throat quiver, her large bosom jiggle. My spine tingled, and I realized that as a small child she had often held me on her lap while she sang.

I sat for a couple of hours in those pews until I felt I had taken my Grandmother into myself. I bought some postcards on the way out. I sent her the one which showed the most awesome space. I wrote, "I have been in here listening for you all afternoon. I think I have heard you, and I am wonderfully amazed."

Lisa and I had dreamed up this trip largely as a way of getting through a stark winter. "I would love to be in London," she would say. I would agree. "And let's go to Ireland," I would say. When I had finally made arrangements for myself, I had used our conversations for my itinerary without any further conscious reasoning for why I was going where.

It was the sense of carrying my Mother around with me that I'd gotten from bumping up against the decorum of British society that made me realize this journey was more research than vacation. I was finished with England, but then I went on to Ireland.

My first walk around Dublin was an exhilarating catharsis. I counted freaks, crazies, drunks, mutterers and leafleters until I lost track. One religious freak even had a mike. All alone on the street corner with glazed eyes and a slit down the back of the armhole of her faded, floral print dress, harking on and on about Jesus, chastising with her pointing finger. Guts, I decided, even if she is crazy.

Whatever it was that brought insanity to the surface there, in Dublin, I was glad of it. I felt soothed by the currents of turbulence surrounding me. I had a room at Mrs. Carberry's with a free electric space heater and I got really good and toasty warm when the sun went down in the evening. The heater was right over the bed and the whole room was no more than six by eight feet and the toilet was on the landing downstairs. And I was content—the people on the streets were upset about one thing or another and they showed it.

It was in that bed, when I woke in the morning, that the voice of Mr. Carberry, down in the dining room, carried up to me as the voice of my Father. I recognized it almost immediately as an illusion. Still, it was so familiar and so long unheard. My Father never had much of an Irish accent, though both of his parents had come from Sligo. It was the inflection, and the tone. I couldn't make out the words, but I could imagine them. He was talking to his wife. It was a simple, morning conversation, a part of their daily routine. He was probably reading the paper at the same time, reading aloud a headline from time to time. Passing a comment as he did. What was it in the tone of those comments that flowed so naturally through my ear drums that it was as if a well worn path already existed there? So natural that I couldn't even identify it. Was it contempt or an edge of irritation or simply boredom? No. Distrust. That was it. The mask for fear that my Father must have felt when he stood, feet planted solid, sighting the rifle on the rabid fox, wanting to hurry up, but also wanting to be sure of getting it right on the first shot. Muttering, "Those damn critters. You just can't trust 'em."

And in the end, when Mother's knife was entering his chest and he finally must have had a flash that it was real—like the afterimage of an echo in your ear when you realize it's your name that's been called over a loudspeaker—what did he think then, in his last moment. "You just can't trust them, anyone." I was sure that's what had gone through his mind.

Because it wasn't just at those moments of real danger that he threw out that conclusion, but in the routine, morning moments too, as he read the headlines. The forces could be as sharply defined as your wife's butcher knife lying on the dish drainer, or nebulous, but either way, you had to watch out. To hold yourself poised with hostility, ready to attack, in order to keep them at bay.

I remembered his face the morning he'd discovered that the brooder had gone out up in the old barn where the new chicks were being raised. When he found them they were all huddled in the corner, and in the process of trying to keep warm that way, they had smothered each other. It was the only time I ever saw tear smudges on his face. The tears were gone by the time I arrived, but his chest heaved and sagged as he counted. He was squatting in the corner, tossing chick after baby, yellow, limp chick from there to the center of the room, counting, "One hundred and ten. . . damn, one hundred and eleven. . . damn," and every damn was a piercing pain being inflicted by that uncontrollable fate that was out to get him, that he couldn't rest from for one minute except by getting drunk and letting the facade fall all around him, letting himself be convinced that during that lapse he could be responsible for nothing. He could do what he wouldn't remember doing. He couldn't be held responsible. He would not be himself.

It was that wondering about him being responsible that reminded me of what he had done to Mother, that gave me a chill so that I had to turn the electric space heater on in spite of the room being oven temperature. And the warmth reminded me of those flannel pajamas I had worn when I was twelve. There I was an ocean away from home, and I was remembering more vividly than ever before the whole scene exposed by the register. His drunken slouch in the arm chair, the way he had slung her name at her, "Laura, c'mere. I want you here." I wasn't sure, but it seemed as if I had never before heard him address her by her name. I tried to think of what he had called her most of the time. "Your Mother" to us. Most of the time I don't think he called her anything.

I remembered her look, sick with obedience like Betty Lou Barnes when Miss Gildersleeve tried to force her to swallow her chili. Betty Lou Barnes had an utter aversion to chili, but that bitch of a second grade teacher said everyone had to eat everything and stared at Betty Lou till she had put all the chili from her plate into her mouth. Still she couldn't swallow, stored it in her cheek like a chipmunk until back in the classroom Miss Gildersleeve called her up to the desk and commanded, "Whatever you have in your mouth, Betty Lou, swallow it right now!" As if she didn't know, while the whole roomful of seven year olds knew not only that it was chili but that if Betty Lou could possibly swallow it she would have done so in the lunch room. Me cringing as Betty Lou's mouth erupted into the trash can, her face turning purple. Me cringing as Mother obeyed, her eyes darting to get away but her body staying put, overpowered, her blood all in her face, her arms useless appendages.

Only in that bed at the Carberry's, rolled up under the comforter, was I sure for the first time that he had managed to hold her there beside him by virtue of his finger or several of his fingers up inside her. I remembered him saying, not sure of the exact words, "Oh, come on now, Laura, enjoy it. You like it, don't you? I can tell. You're getting wet. You're not any better than anyone else, just because you play that thing. You're the same. All you women are the same." I remembered the cruelty in his voice, undisguised, not even slurred, the words slapping against Mother's soft skin like whip stings. Mother, who so carefully picked the hairs from her brush and left them for the birds, Mother, who smiled and stepped back quietly from danger, was not made for his heavy hands. "All you women are the same."

No, no we're not.

I shivered in Mrs. Carberry's bed. I remembered my teeth chattering as Megan had dragged me down the stairs. The waves of nausea rose higher and higher. I tried deep breathing, tried to fight them with calm, but they were too strong, the memory was too strong. I couldn't stop it— Mother's splitting scream. I ran to the bathroom on the landing and heaved all the contents of my stomach. Even when nothing was left, I went on gagging and gagging, sounding like an old, broken washing machine, like Dad on his hangover mornings. I wondered if Mr. and Mrs. Carberry could hear me. I could still hear his voice.

Finally I went back to my room. I ran the cold water and brushed my teeth, over and over, starting with fresh toothpaste each time. They will throw me out for using too much water, I thought. All that flushing (there was no great water pressure in the toilet), all this washing. Then I crawled back in the bed, pulled my knees up to protect the emptiness inside of me and fell into an exhausted sleep.

I woke a short time later, sweating, lost in the tail end of a dream, the white organdy curtains on the window making me think I was back home in my bed in the country, feverish with sunburn; but no, that was years ago. Then, opening my eyes to the heater, I pulled the switch, threw off the comforter and became aware of the slightly rancid taste in my mouth.

I, Francie Kelly, vomited. Vague, my sense of it and the crazy way it had grown enormous, black in my mind to mean death, and there I was beyond it, alive, stroking my damp body in private celebration. Feeling the upward spiral high of knowing I had reached the worst and passed it.

Pangs of appetite for Mrs. Carberry's breakfast brought me downstairs looking like the same person she had rented a room to just the day before.

Only I wasn't.

"Good morning."

"Good morning. You look nice and fresh today," she said.

"Thank you. The room is very comfortable."

FOURTEEN

For my last five days in Ireland I rented a car, drove across to Galway and then went south along the coast. I picked up hitch-hikers all the way, mostly women, occasionally a man and a woman together. I had been feeling very tender since the memory of my father had come in Mrs. Carberry's room, and with the tenderness, came shyness about talking to strangers. The hitch-hikers became my one guarantee of some socialization in the course of a day.

The last day of my car rental I woke in Cobh. I had a full day's drive to Dublin ahead of me, then a flight the next morning. Just past Middleton I came upon a middle-aged woman, a basket on her arm. She walked at the side of the road. I slowed, she turned, her thumb followed her eyes. She reminded me of a cautious aunt. I stopped.

"Where would you be going?" she asked.

"North. Wherever this road goes and then to Dublin."

"I'll take a lift to Youghal, if you don't mind."

"Fine," I said.

She got in. She set the empty basket on her lap and fingered the weave around the edges. It was large and reminded me of a basinet.

"You can put that in the back, if you like," I said.

"Oh no, this is fine. It's only a short way. I'll be doing my shopping in Youghal."

She said she was a farmer, and asked what was I? "A physical therapist," I said. "Physiotherapist, here."

"Ah, what kind of schooling did you have for that?" she asked.

"College. I went to a four year college and I majored in it."

"And your parents? What were they?"

"Chicken farmers," I said.

"Ah," she said, as if she had made a discovery. "You are a smart one. You've got the education. Good for you." She seemed to go on thinking to herself but not talking out loud. Finally she said, "I've got one nephew who has gone for education. Lost. Too bad, you know. It leads to the boy coming home and looking down his nose at us. All the same, it's needed. I'd like more education myself and I'd like some for the priests. They aren't educated to the things people are in need of, just to God. Perhaps they'd know what to do. You know of the National Health Insurance here?"

"Yes, I've heard about it," I said.

"My friend, Nellie, was in for gallstones. They make it sound like everyone gets the same on the National Health Insurance, but it's not so. Those who are on the National only find themselves treated one way—lousy. Those who are paying extra aren't even kept in the same rooms. I was so mad I wanted to write a letter to the newspaper. Times like that I wish I had more education. Then I'd write to the newspaper and tell what it's like."

"I think you should write it to the newspaper just like you told me," I said.

"Oh, no," she said, taking on an air of innocence. She brought her hand to her mouth as if her mouth were a part which had gotten to moving on its own and had best be watched. "I've chewed your ear off," she said, "and we're just around the corner from Youghal."

"Will you have a cup of tea with me when we get there?" I asked.

"Thank you, no. I must get on with my shopping."

She wore sturdy, laced-up shoes and there was a hint of a duck in her walk. She adjusted her basket on her arm and turned to wave just before she rounded the corner and walked on out of sight.

She was my last hitch-hiker. I passed others, but didn't pick them up because I wanted to keep her with me, to let her talk settle down in my mind. For five days I had driven the roads of Ireland with the image of my mother and father steadily in my mind's eye. Although I held them in their moment of collision—perhaps the driving, always the distant horizon with strong sun rays shining through there beyond the clouds, perhaps the soothing rhythm of the ride—whatever the reason, I had begun to experience myself as peaceful, apart from them.

My hitch-hiker didn't settle easily. She had stirred me and left me. I had an impulse to go back and find her, tell her I'd drive her back home after she'd finished her shopping. I'd ask her to talk some more. Of course I couldn't. I had to get the car back to Dublin. I had to go home. My Mother was coming to visit me before the week was out. She had an appointment in New York with an ear specialist to see about her hearing. I had to go back to work, back to living alone, back to the place where I had friends to talk to. Ready or not. I had to talk to Mother. I couldn't have gone much longer talking to myself anyway.

I wished I'd insisted that my hitch-hiker take the time for tea. I didn't even have a head-on view of her in my memory, only a profile—greying hair, braided, the braids looped and pinned on top of her head, sharp cheek bones, a stubborn, large chin, the veins standing out, blue, on the back of her hands.

"Lost. . . too bad, my nephew who has gone for educa-tion." There had been mourning in her tone. I knew the word alienation. She knew that he looked down the nose. That seemed a fairly accurate description of the slant of my vision.

FIFTEEN

I was walking home from work, my gait stiff. I felt as if I were being squeezed. I was in a vise. My head ached, the pressure on the temples. Mother had arrived. She was supplying the push on one side. On the other side I supplied the pressure myself, pushing into her. The reeling gut-knowledge that fluttered in my stomach, wishing simple escape, held me captive. Because of the fluttering I felt I must crank the vise tighter, must keep the headache to remind me it was crucial finally to get things straight with her. Crucial to go home and butt up against her, making myself large and inescapable as a wall, spilling her secret and mine.

I wished I had had a few more days for driving around Ireland or even an extra hour to drop in on Lisa.

I looked up and saw Ben watching me from the other side of Seventh Avenue. Why that day of all days when I hadn't bumped into him in all these months? The traffic light seemed long in changing as we each kept an eye on the other. Then his long strides, the self-conscious, striped-suited legs approached my curb. A quick, friendly kiss to remind me of his soft lips. I noticed he was shorter than he'd appeared in my memories, though still in actuality over six feet.

"Hi. How are you?" I said.

"Pretty well. It's hectic at the office but we have some good jobs."

"I wasn't asking about your job, I was asking about you." I didn't say it. Silence. The discomfort of casual acquaintances standing on the street corner, nothing to lean on. Thinking, but we know each other, *intimately*. Finally saying, "Well, how's everything else?"

"Pretty good. I'm getting along okay." Silence again. There was nothing in him I could connect to. He was staring at me the way he had when we had first gone out together, as if I were a new woman he'd just met and he was considering starting a new relationship. I shifted my weight from foot to foot, as if that would keep him from latching onto me any further.

"How about yourself?" he said.

"I've just come back from Europe."

"Really?" He sounded truly astonished, I suppose because I'd never gone further than Marblehead with him.

"Did you like it?"

"I had a great time."

"You're looking good."

"Actually you've caught me at a bad moment. My Mother's visiting me. She came to see about having her ear operated on. She's gone to the doctor today. . . ."

"Give her my regards."

Whack, whack—his tongue was still a lawn mower blade, cutting off whatever I had to say. I remembered how well we were supposed to know each other, tried again to speak of my distress at being with Mother, but he wasn't listening, only glaring past my eyes with that rude stare of his that never let me in on what he was thinking. I stopped talking and tried to smile to cover the sour taste I had of the aversion coming back to me. "I have to run. She'll be waiting for me," I said.

"It's awfully good to see you again," he said.

I felt myself recoil from the urge to politely agree. "Take care," I said and ran to catch the light before it turned. The traffic moved behind me and my sigh could not be heard over the noise it made. There was nothing in me that wanted any part of him.

I took a deep breath, opened the door and found the apartment empty. Famous Doctor. Mother must've spent the whole afternoon in his waiting room. I lay down on the couch and the temptation to masturbate flickered through my mind, a way to take the edge off the tension. But with the thought came another deep sigh and I felt suddenly calm, the eerie calm of the center of a hurricane. Her suitcase lying open there on my floor, no place really right for it in the whole apartment. For a moment it was a comfort in my state of being utterly alone. Then again it seemed an intrusion and I felt ready for Mother, no need for rehearsals.

I heard the key turning in the lock and instinctively reached for my book, not wanting to be caught in what Mother had always considered to be that disgraceful state of just sitting, doing nothing. Then, realizing it was her dictate, I put the book back down and let her catch me empty handed.

"Hi. How was it?"

"Oh, Dear. I have wonderful news. He wants to do the operation on me. He says I'm the perfect candidate. I have just the problem it's designed to correct."

"Wow, that's great," I said, realizing I'd been wrong all along about her hearing loss. Always thinking mine was one of my inheritances—Grandma Gerty to Mom to me. This meant she didn't have the inherited kind at all. The operation was to unstick the tiny bones. "When are you going to have it done?"

"I have to put in for a reservation for a bed in the hospital. It's elective surgery, you know, so I have to wait. He said maybe six weeks. I'll have to come back then, when they call me."

"Too bad you waited all these years. Gee, you'll never know what you missed in the meantime," I said.

"Well, I don't mind. It's a pretty new procedure. At least now I'll get the benefit of his experience." She sat back, relaxed in the chair. "You know what's such a funny feeling is the idea that something you've lived with for years, that's such a part of you, might be changed."

"Yeah. Remember the day you got your first hearing aid? I was driving you home from the hearing aid store and you kept saying, "What's that ticking noise in the car? Is something wrong?' I told you it was just the normal noise. Then a few days later you said, 'God, you kids make an awful racket that I can't get used to,' and then you started taking it off when you got home from work." I went on in my mind. Why were those people at work so much more worth listening to than your own children?

She took her shoes off and sat with her feet curled up under her. It was a position that conveyed the youth still in her. Also whimsy. Her hair was grey and short and thinning, all the brown luster gone. I couldn't remember how long it had been since she'd worn it in braids like the woman I'd met in Ireland. I had picked up my photographs at noon so I got them out and showed her where I'd been. She studied the pictures long and seriously, first the ones of England, then the Irish ones.

Her body was small and trim, consciously kept to pass through middle age without a spread. The fact of her compactness made it harder to find an opening for saying something I knew was going to unravel her. I had gone back to the couch when she started a second time through on the pictures. I was aware of the sweat on my palms, the clammy cold of my fingers. Moisture glistened in the cracks, my predetermined life lines. The ache in my head had come back to full, booming, thunder pulses.

"Mom, I wanted to tell you about something. I had this weird experience when I was in Ireland." She looked up. "You know how Megan's always had the good memory and mine's always been pretty useless. Well, all of a sudden I developed this sharp memory."

"About what?" She sat straighter. My tension had branched out to electrify the air.

"About the night of the accident." There. She couldn't

tell me not to say it. It was already said. I felt her prickle, but her voice was calm.

"Dear, what do you want to talk about that for? It's so long ago. It's best left alone. It's just one of those things." She closed her eyes and shook her head slowly in the attitude of an apology. In the tone of her voice had been the plea, "Be good, darling. Be quiet."

"Just a minute. I have to get an aspirin," I said. I went in the bathroom. Who was I to overrule her? She was the Mother. She didn't want to talk about it. But I watched myself in the mirror as I took the aspirin and thought—if I let her put me off, if I shake hands and go back to my corner to cower, chances are I'll have a headache for the rest of my life. I took a long gulp of water and went back out.

She hadn't moved in her chair. Seeing how tight her mouth was set, I realized she was scared and the person she was afraid of was me. That touched off a strange sensation in me. I wanted to cry, but I didn't. I wanted to relieve her of her fear, but there was no way to do that. I said, "Mom. . . that night that it happened, I saw. I was down on the floor looking through the register and I saw Dad come in and I saw the way he talked to you and what he did when he had you standing by him."

"What were you doing on the floor?" She looked at me, the accusing, reprimanding Mother, not wholly believing. I kept my eyes fast to hers, fearing I would lose credibility with a side glance.

"I don't know, but I was. I guess because I heard him yell at you."

She covered her face with her hands and bent over, her head down, and we sat in silence, shut out from each other. I watched her hands, the veins on the backs of them, and I saw the collapse of her stiff, usually straight back. First I felt like a spectator, making these observations; then I saw the sorrow in her posture and I felt my throat tighten and ache with her. She looked broken, the way a rag doll looks when you've propped it up and then suddenly it falls forward.

"I'm so ashamed," she said without lifting her head, her voice cracked with pain.

"Don't be," I said, gently, listening to her sobs, feeling them in my own chest, but not knowing what to do, how to be the mother. I got up and went to her chair and sat on the arm of it and still I felt miles away and wondered why we had let ourselves be caught not knowing each other. She was still bent over. I knew I had to touch her but my hands lost volition and wouldn't lift up from my lap to reach out. The precipitous sensation of climbing down a mountain and reaching a ledge I must jump from—only a few feet but my panic enlarges it, my vision of the chasm below sets off gruesome fantasies of an avalanche, my body bouncing off boulders, hurting so bad I cease to feel. I take hold, saying, "Just do it. Jump." My legs bend, preparing to spring, but when they straighten up again, my feet are still right where they were, earthbound. I tottered on the arm of the chair. I reached once, but my hand stopped just short of her shoulder. She still had her hands over her face and didn't know about my problem. I couldn't go on being the voyeur. Finally I got my cold, trembling hand to land on her shoulder.

"I'm sorry," I said. I didn't know what else to say. All the consoling remarks that came to mind were the ones she had used on me, statements such as, "Don't worry about it, it doesn't really matter," or "Calm yourself down, it won't help to cry." And I didn't believe in them.

I said it again. "Mother, I'm sorry."

She brought her head up then and leaned it against my arm. Her face was contorted. I remembered her sitting in the corner that night while we waited for the ambulance, her face blank, not contorted at all. My throat ached and ached and my arm felt stiff, almost painful, where her head leaned into it. "He didn't know what he was doing," she said.

I couldn't agree. I didn't say anything.

"He never really liked me playing the piano," she said.

"I know." Had he done what he had done in any other room, would he still be around, I wondered. It was only the living room that Mother had tried so hard to cordon off as

her private world, her touch of Washington Heights transferred to the country. The floral carpet and the wax smelling
piano and her quiet admiration for the blind piano tuner who
always asked her to play for him when he was finished tuning.
His white stick falling against his black suit as he sank back
into the soft cushions of the sofa. I had often wondered about
the room. As a teenager, I played CLUE, a game that made
us search not only for the murderer but also for the weapon
and the room. While others might have felt the room was
chance, all of my fantasies held its importance as primary.

I was nine years old when a friend of Mother's came to
visit with her little baby and said, "Here, sit right here in this
chair and hold your arms like a cradle and I'll let you hold my
baby. Very careful, now, to support the head. That's just
fine." Minutes and minutes went by. The baby's head grew
so heavy, pushed into my arm, the skull almost bald, hard
bone; my fear of moving all centered there on the point of
greatest pressure. If I moved would the baby's head go bonk
on the hard wood of the table beside my arm?

Mother's head was still in the same place and was burning the bone in my arm, and I didn't dare move. And I had
started this.

She reached around just then and took my arm in both
her hands as if to make sure it was stable. "I remember running into the kitchen and holding onto the sink," she said,
"holding on for dear life because I didn't feel I could stand
on my own feet. I felt so humiliated." As she said humiliated,
she shivered and her shiver went up my arm and then down
my spine. I realized that she sounded exactly like Grandma
Gerty, and even though I couldn't remember Grandma Gerty
ever being humiliated, I knew that she would have said the
word the same way Mom did.

Mom was pressing harder into my arm but instead of
that making my arm hurt worse, it made it feel better. The
pressure was like a salve on my burn.

"I don't know why he couldn't leave well enough
alone," she said.

SIXTEEN

The next morning as Mother and I ate breakfast together, I noticed that her eyes were still slightly puffy, but the corners of her mouth no longer drooped down. We sat quietly for a while but it was a close silence, not the shut-out kind.

"What's to become of you?" she said finally. "Do you think you'll ever get married?"

Her directness took me straight to the answer—"No," which rose, uncensored, to my lips. I was surprised to find out I had made this decision without ever having asked myself that question. "For the time being I'm learning to live here alone," I said. I thought of Mama downstairs with her cats. I thought of Lisa, of Lisa and me bumping around in her kitchen, chopping vegetables for Chinese food. I wanted to see her that evening.

"I'd hate to think that my experience turned you against marriage," she said.

"Don't," I said. "That's not so. It's my experience that's turned me off."

Her face seemed changed, less pained. "I better get my things together," she said.

She put her shoes in last and carefully tucked in the pieces of clothing sticking out the front of the suitcase, then sat on the lid and closed the latches. It was exactly the way I would pack a suitcase, one of those many things I'd forgotten Mother had taught me.

I decided not to go to work but to ride out to the airport with her instead.

"That's not necessary, dear," she said. "I know you just finished using up your vacation."

"I'll take a personal day," I said.

"Well, do as you like, but I'm sure I can find my way alone."

"I know," I said. "I just feel like doing it."

I called my supervisor and told her I wouldn't be in until afternoon. "Guess what I just heard," she said.

"What?"

"Kristin died last night."

"Oh, no."

"Yes. I ran into Doctor Becker on my way in just now. She died in her sleep."

"Oh, oh." Utterances around the sting in the back of my throat. Then, "Good for her. . . I mean doing it in her sleep. Will you find out about the funeral for me?"

"Sure," she said.

The bus pulled out of the East Side Terminal and Mother and I settled back in the high seats. "I was really lucky to have known her," I said.

"What was wrong with her?"

"She had a brain tumor."

I pictured Kristin as I had seen her the first day I had gone to her room, knowing only her name and the medical facts. She had registered in my mind as some sort of an animalistic being as she lay in the white bed of the private room, tubes sprouting from almost every orifice.

Her mother was there and I had introduced myself as Kristin's physical therapist. Her entire head was bandaged, a headdress of gauze and tape. I took her arm, which was pale white with soft skin, and told her I was going to exercise it.

Across the bed on the night stand was a framed picture of a young girl about twelve, athletic and healthy, wearing a school T-shirt. Who was it? My eyes kept wandering back. She grunted and flung her arm out of my grasp. She tried to hit me, but her coordination was off, badly. Mrs. White talked to her, cool and calm on the outside, "Kristin, she's trying to help you. You need these exercises. Try to be good now." I hadn't been able to leave the girl in the picture. It had to be her.

Her mother followed my glance. "She won the broad jump," she said.

I was hot, sweating, and at the same time chilled. She didn't want me to touch her. She was saying something. Her speech was incomprehensible, but I tried. I kept saying, "I don't understand. Say it again." Her mouth worked in expressions of distaste and she spurted explosively. She didn't give up and finally it came out clear: "GET OUT." I was so close to her by then that her saliva spewed onto my face.

Mrs. White, embarrassed, said, "She's been through a lot. She doesn't mean it."

"Don't worry," I said. "I'll leave her alone now. I'll be back tomorrow." But I felt she was evil to the core, mean and ugly and we were in for a long battle in which sooner or later I would reign.

"They only gave her six to twelve months after her operation but it's been three years now," I said to Mom.

"Did you work with her all of that time?"

"Yes."

Every day I had gone back to the battleground, prepared for insult and determined to permit her less and less freedom to get away with her own desires. I forced her to move, to do her exercises, not because I thought it would help her, but because we were caught together in combat. I threatened her in my most authoritative voice. "If you don't move this leg, I'll make you do both arms over again." There wasn't much you could threaten her with. I'd come into her room, saying, "Well, Good Morning, Kristin. Here I am, your favorite person. Are you feeling good and ferocious today?" She would chuckle, a noise that came out through her tracheostomy tube as a series of wheezes and I'd know she was ready for a good fight.

Mom rode along quietly beside me, giving me space for my ruminations. Then she handed me a tissue for the silent tears that had flowed out of the memory and dissolved the ache in my throat a bit.

I'd fought with Kristin all the time in the beginning, but somewhere along the line I'd come to love her. I'd never been able to decipher when the battle had ended and we had begun to look forward to seeing each other. I was only sure that the love had come out of the fight, out of the caring enough to fight.

"Was she in very bad shape?" Mom asked.

"At first she was. Then she had some radiation therapy and she got strong enough to sit up in a wheelchair, but all her hair fell out. She would examine a *Seventeen* magazine cover to cover, trying to decide which was the most attractive hair style pictured. Someone once suggested a wig, but she said, "Yuck, I can't stand phonies." Her mother thought she was saying 'ponies.' Her speech got better so you could understand her on the second or third try. At least I could. She was in the hospital almost a year and then she went home but she still came back a couple of times a week for her exercises."

"How old was she?"

"Fifteen "

"It's a shame," Mother said, and I recognized that statement going over and over in my mind all the time with Kristin. Always it had been there, that lump on the back of her head that looked like half an avocado, that stupid, rotten brain tumor that she had asked me to measure once a week for the past three years.

She had known from the very beginning that she was dying, I was sure. The strange thing was how she had helped me confront it, when it should have been me helping her. Even when she had started getting worse again in the last few months she hadn't expected any pity, just that I should fight with her and tease her and remind her of the battle that we didn't know who'd won.

"I can't explain how, Mom, but what she did was she managed to take the sourness out of death. . . ."

Mother was watching me, concentrating on me, and I think she was trying hard to understand, maybe even was understanding in some silent way that I was talking about the sourness of our lives, too. But she spoke on another level out of habit or perhaps it was out of fear. "Maybe you shouldn't get quite so involved with these people," she said.

"No, Mother. I'm lucky to have known her." The need for giving Mother a lecture on why was gone. She'd have to see and hear whatever she could see and hear for herself.

We hugged before she went to the ticket holders line and the old sense of pained discomfort at this familial display of affection was gone. We were two small, compact bodies, Mother and Daughter. Two women.

"I'm glad we talked," she said.

"So am I."

"And I'm sorry about your patient."

At the funeral I didn't look into the casket. Perhaps they had been able to make her look like the picture again, but I didn't know her that way.

Her mother came to my side. Quietly she said, "It's over."

"Yes," I said. "I'm sorry."

"You were a great help to her in accepting it."

"Thank you," I said, "but I think it was the other way around."

Kristin gone, her teasing eyes gone out, and gone with her, some of the bitterness of my life, because she taught me, played me past my limits, showed me sorrow with a sweet taste.

I went home and searched through the disorderly contents of my desk until I found the picture from her birthday party—Kristin and I, heads together, smiling in defiance of camera fear, just after she had said, "No, I won't smile. You can't make me smile." I pinned it up on my bulletin board.

AFTERWORD

As I write these words in the early fall of 1978 after re-reading a manuscript of GIVE ME YOUR GOOD EAR, I am struck by the fact that there are only four copies of this book in the world, and I am lucky enough to have one of them. By the time you read these words, that luck will be shared because this book will have become a *real* book. It will have been published. But there is another story behind this book and that is the story I want to tell.

Almost a year ago a group of women, including Maureen Brady and myself, shared a weekend in the Rocky Mountains and talked about our lives. Maureen talked about having spent two years trying to find a publisher for GIVE ME YOUR GOOD EAR, her first novel, after having spent almost five years writing it. She was no longer writing on a regular basis, and felt discouraged about ever getting her work in print. We knew that Maureen had been methodically and patiently approaching agents, publishing houses, and the feminist presses about publishing her book, and were amazed that no one had yet decided to publish it.

We were determined that something had to be *done*—no more sitting and waiting. At first we thought the six of us would publish it ourselves, but we live in different parts of the country and soon realized that would be impossible. We then talked more concretely and realistically about the imperative that Maureen publish the novel herself, if that was what was necessary to get the book in print and available for women to read. Someone quoted Judy Grahn, I think, that self-publishing is not an act of defeat, but an act of aggression, and pointed to examples of those few saucy feminists who had already self-published after having received one rejection notice too many, or those who from the outset, for political reasons, had decided to publish themselves. From the energy of that group, Maureen Brady and Judith McDaniel carried that sense of determination over the past year, and created Spinsters, Ink, a feminist publishing house, which marks its first endeavor with the publishing of GIVE ME YOUR GOOD EAR and a monograph by Judith McDaniel, RECONSTITUTING THE WORLD: THE POETRY AND VISION OF ADRIENNE RICH.

However, the celebration of the establishment of another of the welcome but too few feminist publishing houses should not overshadow the story of the debilitating reality with which women writers are faced in trying to be heard. When Maureen told us of all her letters of rejection, we asked her what they meant. She felt they contained definite messages, but she also felt she was too closely invested to be able to analyze them with clarity. I asked her to send them to me because I was curious as to the reasons the presses had given for not publishing GIVE ME YOUR GOOD EAR. After reading these rejection letters (which were often confusing and contradictory) some patterns began to emerge, which I have tried to identify in this essay. Maureen, Judith and I believe that readers should know something of the experiential and political facts of publishing life which made it necessary for this book to be published in this way.

GIVE ME YOUR GOOD EAR received formal rejections from many commercial publishing companies, at least five feminist presses and several New York literary agents. Why? The publishers almost uniformly agreed that Maureen is a talented writer, and a number of publishers, in their rejections, expressed a desire to read her *next* novel. But what are the reasons given in the rejections themselves and what do these reasons really mean?

From the feminist presses the reasons were mostly financial: *The press is very small; our financial and woman power resources are limited. . . . We cannot (for financial reasons) accept full length manuscripts now.* Other feminist presses explained that somehow the book did not fit within the current limited guidelines of the press: *It is a fine novel. . . but is far far far from our limitations (with which I do not wholly agree). That is, there is no stretching this book into a Lesbian novel per se. . . though it is, to quote myself, 'all there for the perceptive reader' and you are right—a coming out scene would ruin it.* From another feminist press: *I think you might be wise to incorporate some coming out experiences into it. After the boldness expressed in Lesbian novels of late, it may have a hard time finding a publisher without a franker approach.* Then there was the press that was devoted to Southern women that year; and the one that was having to limit its production to work by only two women at that time.

The critique coming from the white male commercial presses, while somewhat literary, suggested more concern for Ben than Francie ever did. *Certainly, there are several finely honed, absorbing scenes in the book, but unfortunately, we've decided it would not be a strong candidate for our fiction list. Despite the author's sensitive characterizations and candid presentation of the confusing problems women have to solve, I'm afraid we thought the writing might have been rather less earnest and fresher. The first part of the novel in particular might have been more absorbing had Ben been a less passive, more sympathetic character, and without so many emotionally repetitive scenes between Ben and Francie.* Or from another publishing house: *I didn't care much for Ben—he's portrayed as such a weakling that it's hard to imagine how a strong woman like Francie could have taken up with him in the first place. Even if we reject it, don't get discouraged, a larger trade publisher might well take it on. I would say that its major selling point is that it deals with feminist issues as they affect real people, not just the privileged upper middle class.*

But the comments from the agents, who, after all, are hired to *sell* the book to publishers, are the most telling of how publishers' decisions determine what women have access to read: *Although I admire your work I do not think I would be able to find a publisher for it in this very difficult market.* Or: *I like your writing enormously, but in the last two years or so I have found the market enormously resistant to novels of women's growth and development, of the theme of learning to express anger, of making peace with one's mother, and past. I do not subscribe to the school that these novels are the same; no two people's stories are the same. However, I simply find them impossible to sell.* From another agent: *I would have preferred a more sympathetic character in Ben and a less self-indulgent Francie. Also, I felt that the insights pointed out through Francie's situation, while valid and important, were not enough to set the novel apart in an ever more crowded market of women's novels. If you should decide to apply your considerable talents to a commercial novel, I would be pleased to see it.*

I am writing this essay as a feminist *reader*, one of many whose spirit and intelligence depend on having access to the works of women like Maureen Brady. As feminists, as writers, as readers, we must ask ourselves what these rejections mean from a political perspective. Women have been working to develop a new self-understanding, a growing consciousness which could be the source of radical societal changes. Women's literature is an essential part of developing our sense of female intelligence in the face of white male resistance to those changes. Thus, we must not analyze publishers' rejection letters to women as just another part of the frustration that any creative writer experiences in breaking into the publishing world. We must examine Maureen's experience as one of many examples of white male control. To do so we can ask ourselves: What are the dominant values and assumptions of this culture; and then, how does the publishing world institutionalize these values into operating patterns and practices?

Of the values and assumptions dominant in the publishing world, one is that a novel must be commercial. The commercial press concept of what is marketable in fact largely determines what we read, operating more efficiently than censorship or some other blatant restriction on our constitutional "freedom of expression."* In order to be commercial, it is highly desirable that a novel have sex, violence, or some form of oppression played up throughout its pages. *Give Me Your Good Ear* includes both sex and violence, but the sex is not "hot," and the violence is not violence against women or violence against men by men. The violence is murder/self-defense/justifiable homicide by a woman against a man who has humiliated and violated her. This is clearly not the kind of violence that the male presses find marketable.

A second assumption is that there should be a quota on the number of "women's books" on the market, and that there is a very limited market for "women's books." This is expressed by phrases like: there isn't enough interest in women's novels; or, if you've read one, you've read them all. Note that one agent states that there is an *ever more crowded market of women's novels.* Isn't it obvious that the market is actually crowded with *men's* novels. An extension of this idea is that there is nothing universal about women's literature. *Give Me Your Good Ear* thus is perceived as nothing *substantially more than one woman*'s *personal odyssey*, while a book like *Portnoy's Complaint* is a best seller with "universal significance."

A third assumption is that novels about women should be written in white male terms. Thus Francie rather than

*This should be understood in light of the astounding and revealing fact that the pornography industry in this country (which, for the most part, has constitutional protections) is as large as the recording industry and the film industry combined!

Ben is seen as "self-indulgent" and a publisher is concerned that Ben is not a very *sympathetic character*, that it is *hard to imagine how a strong woman like Francie could have taken up with him in the first place.* Has it not been the experience of many strong women to have taken up with an unsympathetic character like Ben at some point in their lives? Would the novel really have been more *absorbing* (as one publisher suggested) without so many *emotionally repetitive* scenes between Ben and Francie? Possibly. But then wouldn't life itself be more absorbing without so many emotionally repetitive scenes between women and men? One publisher states that the book is too *self-absorbed, that it doesn't offer enough distance on the experience involved, and doesn't really go far enough.* What does this mean? And how far is far enough, anyway? I think it is significant that it is the attitudes and perspectives of the characters that the editors have found objectionable in *Give Me Your Good Ear.* That is because the story is written from a female perspective, and thus is inconsistent with the standards which publishing houses require.

The institutionalized pattern and practice of the commercial publishing world is to reject the work of writers such as Maureen without giving them any clear notion of *why* (other than "it won't sell" or some other idea that blames the writer for being who she is). In addition, the commercial presses offer false hopes to talented writers (*we'd like to see your next novel*) and subtly pressure the writer to change her perspective on life (*if you should decide to apply your considerable talents to a commercial novel, I would be pleased to see it*).

It is interesting to note that all of the excerpts from the rejection letters quoted from above were written by women— women who work near the bottom of the white male publishing hierarchy or who are free-lance agents whose livelihood depends on finding writers to satisfy the needs of the commercial presses. It appears to me that some of these women expressed a great deal of conflict and dismay in rejecting material which they obviously liked on some level, but which their "professional" (white male) instincts tell them will never become a best seller. Their perceptions focus on the limitations of the material itself in relation to male values, without any comments about the assumptions underlying the publishing market.

What, then, is the effect on feminist writers of receiving rejections of their work? It produces anger or, if turned inward, depression, passivity, stagnation. Writers *submit* (a telling word) their work to publishers. Then they wait. As women, we know the strain of waiting, and the resulting sense of powerlessness and anxiety. The history of women is full of examples of novelists like Maureen Brady. The tragedy for all of us is that the works of those women have—as a direct consequence—been lost. And for many women, rejection of their work has meant the end of working itself.

I think it is significant that from the moment that Judith and Maureen decided to stop waiting, to stop submitting, to stop playing the passive role, they freed up that doomed energy and put it into creating the very thing they needed—a feminist publishing house. Their focus changed; they turned to women for financial and moral support, and since have received many, many contributions of money, kind words, and actual work from other women who have felt encouragement and inspiration in the founding of Spinsters, Ink.

So Maureen's story has a happy ending—her book has been published. Many other women share in that happy ending, which marks the beginning, really, of a new venture. Those of us who met in Colorado last year share the pleasure of it, as do those who have contributed to Spinsters, Ink and especially those women whose works are wanting yet to come.

Jacqueline St. Joan
Denver, Colorado

October, 1978

Maureen Brady once again lives in upstate New York, where she spent her childhood. She is a practicing physical therapist and an instructor of physical therapy at Russell Sage College. Her stories have appeared in *Conditions* and *Sinister Wisdom*, and she is one of the founders of Spinsters, Ink, a feminist publishing company.